BERBICE CROSSING

and other stories

BERBICE CROSSING

and other stories

CYRIL DABYDEEN

PEEPAL TREE

First published in Great Britain in 1996
Peepal Tree Press Ltd
17 King's Avenue
Leeds LS6 1QS
Yorkshire
England

ISBN 0 948833 69 6

ACKNOWLEDGEMENTS

Some of these stories appeared in earlier forms in the
following:
'Canary Joe' in *The Fiddlehead* (University of New
Brunswick)
'Across the River' in *The Toronto South Asian Review*
'A Mighty Vision' in *The Canadian Fiction Magazine*
'A Ritual of Fire' in *Kunapipi* (Denmark)
'Methusalah' in *The Northward Journal* (Toronto)
'Antics of the Insane' in *Still Close to the Island*
(Commoner's Publishing, Ottawa 1980)

CONTENTS

THE RASTAFARIAN

Devan stopped and rubbed his eyes. There, in the distance, by the cane-infested canal stood a gaunt, hollow-eyed, straggly-haired man — meagre, as if he hadn't eaten for days. A sadhu, a holy beggarman, all the way from India, maybe. Brother-bhai: Devan was drawn towards him. On the other hand, perhaps it was just someone from a neighbouring village. It was this unholy communistic politics, socialism for the small man they called it, but the people were just getting smaller. It was all the fault of the man they called Lenin. Whenever he saw that face, in book or magazine, Devan quickly looked away — a God-hater! This Lenin who hated all six hundred million Hindus in India!

As he came nearer, Devan could hear the man muttering to himself. Praying. A holy man no doubt. Nearer, Devan wasn't so sure. The man looked dark. A Madrassi, perhaps. A devotee of Kali with his wild hair. Nearer still, the man looked distinctly African. A flutter of alarm. What was a wild-looking African man doing in solidly-Hindu Providence Village?

Now Devan could hear what the man was saying.

'I is I, brethren; I eat no rank t'ing; no fish or flesh of fowl or beast; I only listen to the voice of the One above, the same Jah-Rastafari whose beloved brethren was Brother Bob Marley, whose life ended not far from here, at that place once called

Xamaica. I say, repent and follow the true ways of I-God, Jehovah!'

Devan stepped closer to this gaunt, charcoal-black man.

'Amen-amen-amen!' he was chanting.

Devan blinked a few times as he watched the other's eyes burning deeply in their hollow sockets.

African though he was, this man was evidently a searcher after truth, a man with a sense of the pure. Maybe he could make him a Hindu, if he put his mind to it. Here was a new vision: all the Africans in Godforsaken socialist Guyana becoming Hindus! Some might even go to India on pilgrimages and, much later, go to Africa with their Hindu names, eager to spread the word to Zululand itself. Then the names of the Hindu gods, Ram, Krishna, would be heard in Swahili. Mahatma Gandhi would have been proud!

He laughed, yet the vision awed him. The whole world Hindu. Could such a thing be possible? Dahomey, Ashanti, New York, Washington, London: in time they'd all have genuine Hindu names.

'I is I, sayeth Jah-Rastafari, mon,' intoned the other, eyes closed.

Devan thought of Hinduism going to the very heart of Africa. Ramsingh Livingstone, ha! He wanted to rush forward and embrace the gaunt seeker-after-truth, whose rib-bones jutted out; to tell him about Atman, about living in absolute harmony with the Creator, everyone the world over muttering mantras in their devotion to His Blessed Name and living lives of true piety.

'Is Zion, Brother, here beyond this same river of Babylon, the Land of I and I!' The voice was rhapsodic.

Devan watched him, still gripped by his vision of Hinduism in Africa, though he was beginning to wonder whether this man, so fervent about his own gods, would be quite so easy to convert. But who were Ja and Bredabobmali? Making converts was never easy. He had only to think of his own son, Jotish, the boy who had once collected hibiscus and jasmine for his pujas, now so mannish and scornful.

'Babylon-Babylon,' the incantation rose; 'I and I...'

Devan wasn't sure what to make of this strange mantra, but he recognised the solemnity of a cry from the heart. Now the devotee was puffing smoke from a chillum, like the old Indians smoking bhang, eyes canting skywards as he inhaled deeply, muttering, 'This Blessed Herb that I inhale to keep I and I's spirit clean, cause is de spirit of we own Brother Bob Marley, now one wid Jah-Rastafari-I who lead we outta the white man captivity from this rass-pass Babylon!' And he let out smoke from his mouth and nostrils at the same time.

Suddenly Devan wanted to tell this brother-bhai to stop talking so crazily. He knew these people had been brought to Guyana as slaves, knew the hard times they'd had — the chains, the brandings — but if he learnt to concentrate on Krishna-power and love, maybe he could forgive the European slave-masters, just as the Hindus had done.

But the man looked suddenly aggressive: there was no sweetness in his eyes, maybe because of the bhang he was smoking. Maybe conversion was unnecessary. Perhaps this Jarastafari was really a forgotten Hindu god. Perhaps, he thought, looking at the man's wild, knotty hair, like black snakes coiling, this Jarastafari was a manifestation of Durga or Kali.

Yet fierce as the man looked, inhaling so hard it seemed his lungs would burst, Devan still wanted to befriend him. He had to find someone to talk to about God, under whatever name, in this mundane backwater of Providence Village.

At last the man seemed to have ended his prayers. Devan coughed and started forward, his voice just a nervous whisper.

'You okay, Brother-bhai?' Wind wafted the smells of the bottom-house: incense, resin, cowshit.

'Eh?' came the retort.

'You okay?'

'Move you arse outa me way, I talkin' to Jah-Rastafari by this I-river of Babylon.'

Devan was not to be put off so easily and he smiled nervously.

'You know about Hinduism,' he eventually plucked up the courage to ask.

'Hindooism?'

'Yes.'

'Na... me believe in Jah-Rastafari, I and I only; and I eating no rank t'ing, no fish, no animal flesh; I believe only in de word of Jah-Rastafari-God, mon, same as in Jamaica an' elsewhere in dis Babylon.'

'That alone?'

They looked at each other, and Devan again thought about the man's race, where he'd come from originally... Africa, the 'dark continent' he'd read about, land of the Mau-Mau, people who marauded; tribes armed with spears, attacking... all so bewildering, frightening. Dr Livingstone: what a brave soul he must have been. Livingstone by the Zambezi river, covered with flies, body sheer bones. A darker Africa gripped Devan's mind. Where did this African sleep at night? Where did he get his food?

As if he guessed Devan's thoughts, the Rastafarian said: 'I sleepin' anywhere, under a bridge, on dry ground, on green grass an' mud-flat; anywhere so it clean, cause Jah-Rastafari want me to sleep right here; an' I eatin' what he provideth for me, mon. I go to the vegetable garden next, an' I pick from God's holy ground all that grows in it, that which I can eat: the bananas, breadfruit... and no one shall stop I!'

Devan listened and yet not listened, wondering if somewhere this man had a house — though it didn't seem like it. Suddenly he envied him because he, once again, wanted to be free, though he would never again let Tara know this. He listened to the Rastafarian's words: slow, laboured; looked at the sun glinting on him, his eyes red, his fingers long with the nails uncut and protruding talon-like, his hair knotty, like coiled black snakes ready to spring out. Yet Devan felt something akin to brotherly love, wanted to reach out to touch the knots of hair.

But the brotherly love had evidently not communicated itself to the African who said, 'Look, man, I tell you once; move you arse outa me way.'

This time Devan thought it best to oblige.

When, later, Devan returned home, Tara was waiting outside for him, hands akimbo.

'Where you been?'

'Eh?'

'You been to work?' Her words were brusque: she knew this was unlikely. The calls of the spirit allowed him to work only sporadically.

He wanted to tell her about the black man he'd met, and his spirit of piety and freedom but, as Tara stood obdurately before him, he thought better of it.

Later, though, he could not resist telling her.

Her eyes crinkled, incredulous. 'Ja-rasta-far-i?' She struggled with the word.

He nodded, beaming, encouraging her.

'Yes — a new religion.'

'Not Hindustani?'

'No, African religion — not from India, though who knows.' He chuckled. 'Maybe is we own!'

'Eh?' She had never thought of Africans having a religion of their own, still less one that might be related to Hinduism. They were mostly followers of the white man's religion: Christians — Anglican and Catholic — people who sweated to their churches

in tie and jacket; people who didn't know the ease of the loose
white dhoti. She'd heard of some, 'clap-hand' Christians as
they were mocked in the village, who ranted and raved in
strange tongues. But... a new religion? 'They prappa crazy!' she
fired at Devan.

But Devan continued to tell her about the man's words, about
Jarastafari, and about all things being clean — wasn't that what
the Mahatma had talked about, no? The cowdung-plastered
bottomhouse ... cleanliness next to Godliness, a Hindu precept.
He told her how the follower of Jarastafari had said all things
belonged to a common humanity; not even the vendors in the
market really owned their produce.

Tara's eyes gleamed: 'Oh-ho! That blackman better not
come t'ief my ground provision!'

Devan willed himself not to rebuke her. He would dwell only
on the concept of God, this new avatar, Jarastafari, the river
called Babylon, an ancient source, a place of healing, like the
Ganges itself!

Tara watched him contemptuously, hands still at her waist.
Then she sucked her teeth and walked away, leaving Devan to
reflect on Babylon and Jarastafari... and Breddabob. All men
were the same, in all parts of the world: a true and universal
spirituality existed. At once he called out for Jotish, then the
girls, Shanti and Devi. 'Come, quick. Quick!' he hissed.

No response; only the sound of sucking teeth.

He smiled to himself, benignly.

The next day Devan hurried to the same canal along which
the sugarcane punts were being pulled by sturdy mules or
tractors. Amidst the clanging of chains, the banging together of
the heavy iron punts, Devan thought he heard the loud,
aggressive black people's music from Jamaica which sometimes followed the Indian music played on the early morning
'Indian Hour', with Mohammed Rafi or Lata Mangeshkar.

Affronted, Devan instinctively put his fingers to his ears. Yet he hoped he'd meet the devotee of Jarastafari again.

All the previous night he'd thought about this new religion. Maybe it would take root in this country, perhaps throughout the Caribbean. Maybe this new creed would supplant Communism, but what about Hinduism? Could they coexist? It boggled his mind, the world changing so rapidly.

He turned a bend along the canal and there was the Rastafarian by the side of the water, praying loudly. Devan waved to him encouragingly.

The devotee eyed him surlily, then with a perplexed, half-dazed expression. Devan inched forward. The man looked more wild-headed than ever, smelling of grease, and bhang — which, from the redness of his eyes, he'd doubtless been smoking all night.

The Rastafarian came closer to him.

Devan inhaled a resinous smell, like bark. It seemed to him that the Rastafarian's eyelids whirred like bats' wings as he talked, saliva drying on the corners of his mouth in the heat of the sun. Yes, Devan thought, Africa and India were indeed one; and he must tell the Rastafarian this. He smiled, as the other looked at him askance. Maybe the *Bhagavada Gita* had been read in ancient Africa; maybe this was the source of the Rastafarian's ideas. His heart beat faster: India and Africa as ONE!

The Rastafarian walked to the edge of the canal, slipped into it and began to immerse himself like a pilgrim in the Ganges. Devan listened to him muttering about Jarastafari, as if his entire salvation depended on it.

'Come, bredder, I go sprinkle water on you, same as Jah-Rastafari order me to do, to make you a convert of the true religion Emperor Haile Selassie now proclaims across this land dat one Sir Walter Raleigh turn into dis Babylon. Yeah, you an' all the others could be like Brother Bob Marley, finally going

to the land of Ethiopia, the real Zion — to behold the spirit of
the Lion of Judah!'

Devan remained at the water's edge, the smell of rotten cane,
dead fish, rusted sardine cans, rags soaked for months rankling
in his nostrils. The sun beat down on him. He was beside the
Ganges, the ancient river, garlanded; lily and hibiscus flowers
round his neck; all burdens lifted; cleansed of fleshly desires,
all that was impure. The two of them, he and this Bob-Marley-
Brother in Providence Village... and the life of desire, the
senses, would be gone once and for all. Maybe then the two of
them could go from house to house and PROCLAIM THE
ANCIENT HINDU-RASTAFARIAN-INDIA-AFRICA RELI-
GION! He imagined the face of Lenin. Yes, their combined
religion would fight off that God-hating force! All men and
women would soon be free to choose their own destinies.

The Rastafarian beckoned to him, and smiled.

Devan smiled back.

The Rastafarian stretched out a hand, preparing to pull
Devan into Zion's crystal stream.

Devan hesitated as he saw the bloated carcass of a dog
floating downstream, though he reflected that the Ganges was
not clean in the conventional sense but was yet a place of
purification, a place to be freed from all past evils, lusts of the
body, the vile senses which continually plagued him (though he
had to be careful not to let Tara know this). At the thought of
Tara he began to reflect that it was most unlikely that the
Rastafarian was burdened with a wife. What freedom it would
be for the two of them, pilgrims after truth, to wander in the
wilderness together for forty days and forty nights!

The Rastaman eyed Devan sharply, evidently put out that
his fellow pilgrim showed no inclination to take the proffered
hand and cleanse himself.

Devan, instead, was imagining the two of them going everywhere in the Caribbean, then to Miami, New York, Toronto —

where many Africans and Indians lived in mutual distrust. There they would make converts, telling their followers that this was how it was meant to be, that Hinduism — the mother of all religions (including Judaism, which was why Jesus lived eighteen years in India as a sanyasi) — had now spawned something new: the combined forces inspired by Zion and the Ganges; and how with One Love the world would be saved.

But then he imagined Tara raging at him as she'd done when he'd tried this before, when she'd taken the children and left the house. He didn't want that to happen again. Suddenly he wanted to get away from the fetid canal.

But the Rastafarian stretched out a claw of a hand, grabbing him.

'Welcome to Zion, Brother! Welcome to Zion!'

'Eh?'

'The land of holiness an' blessedness. We shall now be free.'

'Free?'

'Slavery is over, mon.'

Devan, though, wasn't registering anything as the heat slapped against his face. He was still thinking about Tara.

'Yes, Brother, me glad you come to join me — a true island-prophet.'

'Prophet?'

'Together we shall change de spirit o' dis land. I will lead you 'cause black people come here first, before Indian people. But now we'll return to Zion as one, to be in the land of Judah. Yes, we shall walk through the desert together!'

'Desert?' Devan started to become afraid, thinking of dry fields, whirling winds.

'Yes, Brudda, the Lion of Judah will personally welcome his true disciples in Africa!'

Devan felt a sprinkle of water from the mud-brown canal falling on him. He wanted to be away from this tentacle of a hand gripping his wrist.

He tried to pull back, but the Rastafarian gripped him harder, muttering: 'We shall be free from the slavery that has overtaken the world, the greed and lust. Is why Jah bring you to me.'

'Not Krishna?'

'You go be my first follower; I, the Prophet, after Emperor Haile Selassie and Brother Bob Marley. We shall swim together in this river of Babylon.'

Devan was terrified; he couldn't swim.

The Rastafarian kept talking, his vice-like grip stronger, his eyes aflame, his dreadlocks flying out like snakes.

Feeling dizzy, Devan closed his eyes and mouthed the name of Krishna as a mantra. When he opened his eyes again, he saw someone else, a woman, darker than Tara, and definitely kinky-haired. She stood on the bank of the canal, hands on her large hips. She looked so striking, more powerful than any woman he'd ever seen.

Suddenly she let out, 'Herbie, is what de ass you doing in that filthy canal water, eh? Is where you been all dese past two days that I been looking out for you, searching night an day? You forget de chil'ren wondering where dey father gone!'

The words rose shrill. Devan couldn't keep his eyes from the woman's breasts rising, falling; hands lifted in the air, as she continued in her wrath.

'March yuh ass outa there — if you think you is a man! March out an' stop playing de fool! And go back an' cut cane, cause that's you all you good for!'

Devan looked at the Rastafarian-Brother-called-Herbie, whose eyes were downcast, whose teeth chattered. This was a moment of real travail, and Devan felt for him. Then he turned to look at the woman on the bank, a real handsome-faced black-African woman. What did skin colour matter?

The woman was still bawling out:

'Yes, Herbie , de chil'ren starving, an' you playin' de ass by this nasty canal wid dis coolieman, thinking you's in blasted Africa. But you in Guyana, see! Haile Selassie done dead... And people in Ethiopia starving, so why the hell you don't move you crazy-arse self outa dere!'

Then she started pulling at her husband's arms, as if she were pulling out a tree-stump from the hard ground. Brother Herbie-the-Prophet was succumbing, his bare feet, caked with mud, starting to follow the woman.

'We need money to buy a radio and video, 'cause the children want to have fun too! And me need perfume and lipstick — just like women in America and England! And me want to own things like Indian people — an' not be poorarse-black forever! So we got to hustle for weself. So go back to the canefield, see!'

Then the woman turned around and looked at Devan.

He forced a smile, his eyes still magnetised to the upwards and downwards movements of her breasts.

'Who is you, eh?' she asked in the same loud tone. 'You is a kiss-me-arse coolie Rastaman or just a grinning fool?'

Devan started to explain that, well, no, he was a Hindu, but she fixed him with such a contemptuous look that he stuttered into silence.

'Well, whatever you is, you could pray for he then, eh? Pray for my husband Herbie to save himf from straying, if you is some kind of holy man.'

Devan smiled, searching for an answer to give to this beautiful woman, but just as he started moving towards her, he saw Tara coming, eyes blazing, glaring down on him...

'Devan! Devan!'

The African woman was laughing loudly, as if she'd planned it all along with Tara; began laughing at him as no one had ever laughed at him before.

Absolutely no one!

Blasted Rastaman!

CANARY JOE

I say to Joe 'You see, is no good you talking like this.' Joe eyes
me and winks, his face like an iguana's. He begins laughing
and I know he's in a really good mood. Just like Joe, I say to
myself. But I also sense that he knows there's a bird in the air.
I look left and right; the others are looking too, while Joe
nonchalantly eyes his decoy bird in the cage on top of the
bamboo pole.

We're looking in every direction, waiting for the moment the
new bird will come and sit plumb on the sticky balatta gum that
Joe's put there as a snare.

Joe suddenly 'sees' it, in make-believe, a bird coming out of
the sky, wings whirring. He smiles; it's his bird all right. This
bird's a real whistler! He's done it again, and he'll be asking
thirty or forty dollars for it. Joe has a knack with the birds.

Joe grins 'cause he knows what I am thinking. Then he
begins whistling hard, as if imitating this invisible bird in the
air; the boys come around and begin whistling too. Joe whistles
harder, and they stop and watch him, spellbound. Now there's
a mammoth whir in the air, as if a dozen birds are vying all at
once to get on top of the balatta snare. Joe claps his hands once
or twice, whistling even harder; then a low, soft sound comes
from his lips, and he's not looking at us any longer.

One man moves up closer to Joe and says, 'Stop your whist-lin', Birdman. Stop it now.' But it's as if Joe's deaf; he starts calling this special bird, kurru-kurru, such a strange, sweet sound, his lips puckering, the word coming out in a soft trill.

'Yeah, stop it!' the boys holler, and some, mesmerized, begin dancing around him, as if the bird in the air is making them do this.

Joe mumbles something about his sweet joy, 'cause he fig-ures this bird will make him rich. Then he looks at me oddly, grimacing, like there's a strange pain in his throat going down to his stomach and the rest of his body. At once everyone starts hearing a louder flutter. They look left and right, and Joe's own bird begins to do a dance in the cage, fluttering its wings and screeching — the dance everyone's been waiting for.

There's a loud whirring in the air, then absolute silence broken only when the boys start calling out, 'Is when you go stop playing de fool? Hey, Canary-Joe, you think you go whistle like dat all you' life?'

But Joe closes his eyes, smiling in sweet oblivion.

Now all ah we getting impatient 'cause it seems that no bird is coming. If only Joe would stop smiling and shaking his head. But I done say that birds have a way of knowing things which a man, who cannot fly, can never really tell. Yeah, that's what I heard Joe himself say once.

When Joe starts whistling again, it causes the bird in the cage to whistle too, and soon everyone's whistling, involved in the act of catching this still invisible bird. Arms go up and down, shoulders wriggle, mouths puckering all the while. In the resinous air, the bamboo pole, sticky with balatta, seems to waver in the heat.

The Birdman smiles.

I move closer to him and say, 'Joe-man, wha' kinda bird is it? You have to tell we.' I figure Joe already knows. But he shrugs.

'Wha' is it, Joe?' I ask again. But he only rolls his eyes. All this time the invisible bird is drawing closer; a stronger flutter of wings; we can even breathe the presence of this strange bird now.

'Is it really coming, Joe?' someone calls.

'Yes, it's coming, like a message from God on high,' Joe replies.

Then everyone closes their eyes in an expectant hush, but still nothing happens. I close my eyes tighter, though I know Joe has his open. He's really nervous, I can tell. We're all waiting for that bird, willing it to make its grand entrance to join the other bird in Joe's prison-cage.

Then it's as if the two birds are whistling, two birds as one — like God's holy spirit.

I close my eyes tighter.

'Whistle on, bird,' I say to myself. Then I open my eyes to see Joe smiling, though the atmosphere is solemn, like Biblical times.

One man says softly, 'Amen. That indeed's a bird of God!'

I suppose it's from then that folk start seeing Joe as having strange powers. It's the way he carries himself too, wagging his head like a horse or dog, talking to himself, muttering words of wisdom.

Men having problems with their womenfolk start coming to see Joe, and he develops a knack for telling them all sorts of things, though not before first consulting his new bird: this same bird which he keeps calling with a different name each time, as though it is indeed the bird of God.

'What's botherin' you now?' Joe asks the next visitor; then he turns to his bird and asks: 'Say, what ails this creature of God? Come'n, Simon, tell me dat.'

The bird in the cage whistles a reply, though not before Joe starts saying kurru-kurru under his breath. Then Joe turns to the fella again and mutters something about having eternal faith in the powers that control the universe, which no one else in the world has knowledge of but he!

'Amen, amen!'

Another man comes to him, and Joe turns to his bird, calling it Luke, then John... as if he's short on memory; and each time he'll wait for the bird to whistle after making that kurru-kurru sound; while the man heaves in anxiously, expecting a miracle to happen. Then Joe starts talking about higher powers, preaching like a hot gospeller for all to hear.

'Amen, amen,' the words resound: the expectation of real blessings from on high.

Before long the rumour starts spreading that this bird in the cage is from another land, an ancient place which no one has ever heard of before. Even I start seeing in this bird's eyes things I've never seen before: something human, with real spirit and all.

Joe comes up to me, and he knows what I am thinking.

'You got to believe.'

I nod.

'It's a real miracle-worker,' he tells us; ' it can call up other birds out of the deep blue sky to take its place. An' birds from the jungle, too; an' birds from the sea.'

People repeat these things to one another, some referring to Joe as God's own ornithologist, though he can hardly read or write. He now seems a sort of genius among us, who's really seeing things because of the inspiration that comes to a man devoted to such a special thing as a bird.

But the more extravagant the claims made about Joe, the more I remember how we used to mock him, as if he was a weird sort who'd come to no good. I can't help feeling suspicious as I watch him now, solemnly muttering about how valuable this bird is, and how he could sell it to anyone who wants to work miracles and tell fortunes and the like; and yes, you could make the sick heal and someone fall in love at the wink of an eye, all owing to this bird.   .

Joe looks very serious, eyes hardening, like small leaden balls, and no longer rolling about as if he's crazy. Sometimes I look into those same leaden eyes, and then at the bird in the cage — and it's as if I am seeing the same thing.

Eh-eh, I look around at everyone marvelling at this same ordinary bird in the cage, which no longer seems able to whistle or attract another bird from the sky. An idea strikes me right then, and I say to Joe, 'I want to buy your bird.'

Joe laughs (sort of). 'You do, man?'

'Yeah,' I say.

'You have five hundred bucks?'

Maybe Joe doesn't know my circumstances, even though we've known each other a long time now.

I nod.

Joe grins.

'Sure, I have, man,' I say.

Others, overhearing us, gather around. Joe starts laughing as he looks at his bird, which now appears really sick — to me at least... Maybe it's sick on account of all the excitement and attention it's been getting. I look at its hardening eyes and suspect that Joe must have given the bird something to drink, which is causing all this to happen. Yeah, this bird Joe's so eager to sell will soon die.

'Where's your five hundred then, man?' he demands.

'At home, Joe,' I say.

'You have that amount o' money at home?'

'Sure Joe,' I say. 'My ma's been keeping it for me.' I'm sure Joe knows I am lying, as much as I know he's also lying about the bird. The others are watching us, gawking. Joe starts saying how some folks are really strange; how there's this one for-eigner, an American (or a Canadian), who has made him an offer of one thousand dollars for this same bird!

Gasps all around. That kind of money is a real fortune.

Joe watches me and grins.

Now I'm sure he's looking for a way out of selling me the bird. Yeah, he knows I'm calling his bluff, that I've seen through his 'holiness'. But Joe has guile; I've known him long enough.

A few days go by, and each time there's a lot of gaffing between us. Joe says he'll hold onto my offer, but there's a better one on its way that he'll have to consider. I look closely at the bird again, wanting him to think I really believe it's a miracle-bird! But what I see is a bird limping on its right leg, a really sick bird.

I ask, 'Can your bird really whistle, Joe?'

'That bird will only whistle to tell a fortune.'

I look again at the bird's leaden eyes.

Everyone's getting into the act now; and a bid is taking place: people suddenly turn rich, hoarding money all these years. At the same time, we're waiting for some wealthy foreigner to come along to outbid us, a German, Swede, Frenchman, Dutchman... even a Canadian willing to take up the challenge!

Joe's own eyes become more leaden each day. I know then he's desperately hoping for that one special bird from the air to appear. This truly miraculous bird will fetch two thousand dollars, which one of these same foreigners will be only too glad to pay.

'Kurru-kurru,' Joe calls under his breath, looking around, twisting-squirming.

Another week goes by, and no new bird appears. Joe keeps saying it's coming from really faraway: a place called Siberia. All this time the bird in the cage rolls its leaden eyes and looks at us ever more mournfully.

I begin to think that Joe can't wait, that he'll have to go out looking for a replacement; he'll have to go deep into the forests away from the coastland, even into the hinterland where rumour has it that birds are abundant.

But Joe seems even more determined to deny the realities, now demanding three thousand dollars for this same half-dead bird.

'Think of the afterlife, brothers,' he calls out. 'It's sheer bliss. My bird's been there, and is now back. Look at him good, and you'll see it in his eyes. And when you go there through my bird, you'll get away from this land of perpetual blight. This bird's going to take you to the white man's paradise, his land on high, across the sea and ocean, the land so full of milk an' honey; this land of peace and opportunity, brothers! Put all your money together, I urge you...'

More folks are coming by, watching. Joe is now truly inspired, his eyes rolling up as he rants and raves: 'Yes, this is the bird of everlasting life! Put your hands in your pockets, four-five-six of you. Dig deep into your flesh and fork it out, brethren! Pool together and make an offering to God on High!'

I think that if the bird lasts out the night, maybe it will indeed be a miracle.

The next morning Joe appears, alone, the empty cage in his hand, looking grim. All ah we gather round him, eager, disturbed.

'Where's the bird, Joe?'

Joe merely shrugs.

'What have you done with the bird, Joe?' I ask.

'It's sold.'

'Sold?'

'For how much?'

'A dollar.'

The crowd sighs.

'But that bird's worth five thousand!' someone cries out.

'It's the best bird from these parts,' another calls, as if in some way it belonged to all of us.

Everyone's aghast, angry as they repeat these words.

Joe just keeps nodding strangely, not looking anyone in the eye; only looking at me sideways, as if I am the only one who understands what has happened.

I say: ' Joe, I done know the bird's dead.'

He lowers his head.

After a while he begins talking: 'Yeah, I got rid of it, give it away, man — jus' like dat.'

All ah we waiting for Joe to say more: to say why he has given away this special bird, half-dead as it was, and now indeed dead, as I suspect.

Looking at Joe again, I anticipate right then he will start whistling as I've never heard him whistle before. And he does, and he's like a bird himself, his dead bird, as if that bird's been reborn in his mournful voice, and his whistling seems to bring out a flutter and whir in the air like a mighty visitation!

Everyone put their hands to their ears, marvelling at what's happening. One or two start to smile, 'cause they've been expecting this to happen, haven't they?

Joe starts telling us how he gave away the bird to a white man from a real foreign sounding place — Xanadu? — that he says is in Africa, but only white men know about this place of paradise, which all other men on this earth — black and brown and yellow — will never be able to find; which was why it was only right for this whiteman to take such a bird back to the land of yonder.

Then Joe starts whistling again, with a sound so loud it is deafening.

I put my hands to my ears and close my eyes, feeling dizzy. Yet the sound continues, the tune loud and clear.

Now I put my hands in front of my eyes, screening the onslaught of birds which seem to be coming from everywhere.

Immediately a bird lights on top of the cage and is stuck on the balatta for all to see... A bright new bird, vibrant, really alive! And it starts singing its special song as Joe stops whistling.

They're all Joe's confirmed disciples now. This miracle has happened before their eyes. Fellas start putting all their money before him, pooling it together.

This bird is really singing. Listening is believing, I say, and I can't decide whether Canary Joe has pulled his biggest trick on me yet, or whether I am really hearing what sounds like a real choir from on high. I nearly find myself doing the same as the rest of them, but figure I will have to catch him another time.

ACROSS THE RIVER AND INTO THE TREE

The axe bit deeper into the wood as the old man grunted, heaving in again and swinging once more at the tree. Then he looked across the narrow river at the youths idling there. He swung again, a mightier whack this time, the sound echoing far across the village. Face taut, he seemed bent on chopping down the silk-cotton tree.

The youths liming out at the shop across the river watched the axe rising and falling, bark flying in all directions, falling in the river, ripples widening close to the lotus leaf-pads. One youth imagined the tree coming down with a mighty splash. Why did he have to cut it down? It had been there as long as he could remember.

The old man, nose ridging his face, eyes like a hawk's, maybe he wanted to show them what their ancestry was all about; what hard work was really like.

He heaved again.

'Look at he good! He's crazy!'

'He'll do that 'till he drop dead!'

They watched the sweat dripping down his leather-hard back; their gaze shifting to the water glistening where the sun's rays fell.

They knew Jehangir was perhaps the last of the line, born in the subcontinent, a place unknown to them, a place of strange lore, the traditions of their parents, even more so of their grandparents.

They looked curiously at Haroon, one of their group, because they knew he had a keen interest in the old man's granddaughter, Bibi. She was hidden away in the small house not far distant, but the river between them made it seem as if deliberately beyond their reach.

Haroon was indeed watching the old man, and then beyond him the house.

The others clapped cards and laughed noisily.

Haroon studied a particular ripple, a piece of bark flying far from the axe. Bibi was so beautiful. He watched as Jehangir paused to wipe the sweat from his face. Had the old man turned to look towards Bibi's house, and was that a glare of recognition he was fixing on him? Did he suspect something?

'Is true he really come from India?' a youth asked. The question hung in the air. The sun's heat was now overbearing. Haroon wiped a film of sweat from his neck.

'He old. Yet he so strong.'

'Is a tree he cuttin', not sugar cane!'

Haroon looked away, embarrassed by their lack of respect for the old man.

Later in the day, as it grew darker, Haroon continued looking across the river, at the tree and the house beyond it. Maybe it'd rain before long; there were clouds piling. Would Bibi, with her long, braided hair, supple limbs and the lovely dark eyes he wanted to look into for the rest of his life, would she come out now across the bridge to fetch water from the artesian well?

She was only sixteen, he one year older.

Next morning, Bibi rolled up the roti she had made and put them into the aluminium container for Rasoul, her father.

He came into the kitchen, thinking of the day's work ahead:

ploughing the rice field and taking care of his few heads of
cattle. Bibi smiled at him, hands resting on her small waist. She
was so much like her late mother, Rasoul thought: her face fair,
her hair jet black. Her morning smiles were always an inspiration. Ah, one day she'd be married, she wouldn't be around
much longer.

Bibi fussed over her father, laughing. They heard the old
man's voice, calling out his prayers to Allah, a sound to arouse
all Muslim consciences. It was the old man who was pressing
that Bibi should leave the house, that it was time she married.
A month ago the old man had warned Rasoul: 'Look out for she!'
What had he meant? Rasoul had laughed then. It struck him
now that it had been around the same time the old man had
started chopping down the tree.

'But she only sixteen; she too young,' he had argued.

'Never mind dat; she must!' That was his father, always so
uncompromising.

Rasoul looked at Bibi again: he'd take the image of her face
with him to the savannah as he ploughed the land, talked to the
cattle.

'Maybe you not go out today, Pa?' she said.

Rasoul patted her hand. 'I must.'

'You always work so hard.'

'Yes, jus' like my father. You see he outside already,
chopping that tree again.'

Bibi smiled, but with a tremor she hoped her father hadn't
seen. She wasn't sure what her father's reaction would be if she
told him what she felt for Haroon, but as for the old man, she was
definitely afraid of him.

As Rasoul ate the food Bibi put before him, he wistfully
recalled her mother telling him in her dying moments that he
must always look after their daughter. Shamoon had been gone
from his life for three years now, following her sudden illness.

The sunlight was just coming in through the window in

luminous strips as Bibi watched her father leave the house.
There was the old man hard at work; by the shop the youths had
already gathered: Boyo, Latif, Anand... Haroon!

Later that morning, Haroon watched Bibi set out with a pail
in her hand across the bridge, her long hair fluttering in the
wind. Would she find his letter? He wished they could simply
talk: he'd tell her all his deepest feelings – maybe she too.

He looked on anxiously as she nervously glanced around and
then bent down at the far end of the bridge to pick up the note.
She looked at the paper, then crumpled it in her palm. Lowering
her head, she walked on.

Haroon smiled, satisfied.

The other youths also watched Bibi's hips swaying as she
walked. They knew how lovelorn Haroon was, how much he was
attracted to Bibi: her waist, the bulge of her breasts, dark
nipples under the pink dress which clung to her body, almost
translucent in the sun. There was definitely something going on
between them: Bibi's continual coming to the well, seemingly
so shy; Haroon, hair neatly combed back with vaseline, like
Elvis Presley, never failing to be at the shop.

Bibi hurried back across the bridge, trembling with anxiety,
the letter a crumpled ball in her hand. Had the old man seen her
pick it up?

She knew Haroon was watching her, wanting her. Once
inside the house, she was more at ease. From a chink in the
jalousie, she looked out, clutching the note. It was written on
brown paper, a crust of sugar still on it: paper which Haroon
must have torn from a sugar-bag. A tear started coming down
her left cheek; she wasn't sure if it was of joy or frustration.
Quickly wiping it away, she once more looked at the old man:
saw how much more he'd cut into the tree; it would be down
soon. She wanted to be close to Haroon, now. Did it have to wait
until the night? Why did the river have to separate them?

Water swirled; more chips of wood flew in the air; the leaves suddenly shrilled in a gust of wind; the doors, windows and zinc sheets of the houses shook, rattling hard.

It was already dark when Rasoul returned home from the fields, exhausted. He went straight to the river and started washing away the grime from his hands, feet, neck and face; he wanted Bibi to see him very clean, always. He laughed to himself, thanking God for giving him such a lovely, dutiful daughter. Then he saw the old man approaching him, something on his mind.

'Wha' is it, Pa?'

'She mus' marry.'

'Why the hurry?'

'She mus'!' Jehangir too bent down to the river and splashed water over himself.

Rasoul looked at the tree, saw how deep the cut was: only a little more and it would fall. He was amazed and not a little alarmed at the energy and will his father still had.

'A wedding'll take time to arrange,' he muttered. 'I got to make a match, a suitable one. I have to talk to the relatives, so many of them.'

'No time to wait,' growled Jehangir, hollow-eyed.

'Wha' de matter wid you?' Rasoul hissed, no longer washing, looking across the river to the houses, the shop; then at the tree once more.

The old man's face stiffened. Blood rushed to the capillaries in his cheeks and neck. His eyes blinked rapidly as he stuttered hoarsely, 'You... you, refuse to tek my advice. You go be sorry.'

'What you talkin' 'bout, Pa?'

The old man got up, and late as it was, hurried to the tree and once more started hitting at it with the axe; the blade biting deep into its bone and marrow. Leprous-looking shards of bark and pith, some as thick as tarpaulin, flew everywhere. Again and again he hit out, as if he would never tire. Rasoul shuddered as he watched his father. The tree suddenly seemed to lean to one side, the axe wedged into it.

Rasoul wanted to tell his father to stop, but the old man's will was so fierce that Rasoul only watched, awed. Another piece of wood splashed into the water. Rasoul remembered watching dogfish, a dozen or so, tearing into a dead fowl floating there, pulling chunks of flesh like cotton wool from it. What had brought back that disgusting memory?

He got up and walked swiftly to the house. Bibi, the letter still crumpled tightly in her palm, came to him. She had heard the old man's harsh tone and guessed what he must have been saying. Yet she was taken aback by her father's abruptness.

'You got to marry soon.'

'Eh?'

'You heard me.' He raised his voice, with a sternness she was not used to hearing.

'But...' She was at a loss for words, dismayed. How could she persuade him she didn't want an arranged marriage, that she wanted only Haroon. She held the note even tighter in her hand. Resentment flooded into her: *Let the tree fall on the stupid old man and kill him*. But no sooner had Bibi thought this she was ashamed and shocked at herself, because she loved her grand-father, whiny and querulous though he often was.

'What's that you got?' Rasoul demanded.

'Wha' you talkin' 'bout?' Bibi's thoughts were in disarray.

'What you hiding in you hand.'

Bibi's stomach turned; she lowered her head, unable to meet his eye. How did he know? Had the old man told him?

Jehangir entered the house, growling: 'Me na dead yet.'

Rasoul looked from his daughter to his father.

'Wha' you talkin' bout, Pa?' Rasoul asked irritably.

'Me na dead yet.'

Rasoul went to the window and looked out at the tree in the dim moonlight. It would soon be an unusually large moon, leaves shimmering in its light, its reflection in the river. He was hypnotised by the sight, so lovely, wondrous. Again he started thinking about his late wife.

Bibi stood close to him, silent, feeling remorse over the signs of her father's distress.

The old man growled again, 'Me na dead yet,' as he sat on the bare floor, his head lowered into his hands, as if in an act of obeisance.

Rasoul and Bibi watched the old man until he lapsed into silence and then lay down to sleep. Neither could think of what to say to the other, and, wrapped in their own thoughts, they gazed out into the moon's pallid face, the tree's reflection in the water, leaves like jewels.

At about ten o'clock that night, as the stars dimmed, Haroon determinedly but nervously walked across the bridge. A heavier gust of wind threatened an imminent storm. The boys at the shop had talked about the weather building up, the rainy season beginning earlier than usual. Soon the cane cutting would begin and, for a time, they would have work. One had said to Haroon, 'Wha' 'bout you – you go start workin' wid us?'

'Maybe,' he had said. But Haroon had other plans flitting through his mind.

He stepped more carefully as the bridge shook. He recalled the boys' taunts: 'Maybe you'll marry Bibi, if the old man first agree!' He'd denied any infatuation with her but they had jeered, 'We see how you giving she the eye. But that ole man, ha, he too old-fashioned; he believe in parents making a choice for she!'

Another tentative step in the semi-darkness; the water below; the giant tree like a sentinel watching him. Would Bibi be waiting?

He looked up. The moon seemed closer, coming down from its balcony of clouds, as if it would suddenly start chasing him across the bridge. He was afraid, half-wishing he hadn't written the note. He looked at the tree, heard the ghost of the old man's chopping, that thud, like a mammoth heart beating.

He stumbled, nearly fell, but recovered quickly and got safely across. As he moved closer to the house, it was so quiet that he feared any slight noise would attract attention.

Bibi opened the door to his light knock, heart pounding.

'You ready?' he whispered.

'Yes.' She hesitated, then said, 'Here, tek me bag.'

He took it, held her hand, felt her fingers trembling. He had to prove himself strong, despite how he felt.

'You okay?' he asked.

She nodded, wanted to ask him the same...if he was *really* okay.

They set off across the bridge, away from the house, treading carefully. Leaves rustled, filling their ears, Bibi's in particular. She was doing something which made her head spin, this disobedience, which was yet an assertion of herself, of who she was. She kept looking back, wanting to cry, because she was leaving the old man and her father. Suddenly she didn't want to go anymore.

Haroon gripped her hand, but she stopped in the middle of the bridge. 'Wha's the matter?' he asked.

'Nothing.'

'You sure?'

She didn't want to tell him she was afraid, didn't want to go through with their plan. She was thinking of her mother – if only she were here now. Would her father have ordered her to marry at the old man's insistence if her mother had still been alive?

Just then they heard a faint cracking, the noise growing louder, carried by the rising wind.

'Wha's it, Haroon?' Bibi blurted out.

'Is de wind.'

'No, is something else!'

The sound grew louder.

'Oh God!' he cried, 'Is de tree!'

It was falling into the river right across the narrow bridge, towards them.

'Oh God!'

Haroon gripped her hand, pulling her back towards the house, his fear galvanising him.

'Run, run!' he yelled, pulling her harder.

They heard it: a mighty crash, water rising everywhere, leaves and branches tumbling, crashing, rising-falling in every direction; the ground rumbling beneath their feet.

Inside the house, the old man stirred; fevered in his bones.

'Me na dead yet,' he muttered. He heard the sound, the water rising up in mighty waves and he was suddenly in a ship rocking in storm-tossed seas, on Kali Pani, leaving India. He could not escape this sensation. What made him feel this way?

'God, help me, son. Whe' you is? Bibi, child, whe'?'

Stiffness clotted his veins, rising up from his hands and feet. 'Me na dead yet,' he cried again hoarsely.

Bibi and Haroon clung to each other like entangled vines; the branches of the tree spread out in the moonlight across the river; it looked larger now than it had when standing, the river narrower.

Others came running, aroused by the sound, eager to find out what had happened. The tree across the river! Someone near Haroon said, 'Did it wake you too, eh?'

Haroon turned, saw Bibi's father close by, though he seemed not to mind that Bibi clung to him.

Rasoul, coming to his senses, asked Bibi: 'Where's de old man?'

'Yes – where is he?' Bibi shrieked.

'Maybe he inside the house,' Haroon said.

Rasoul went back into the house, Haroon and Bibi following him closely.

Inside they saw Jehangir on the floor, where he usually slept, but crouched, buckled in a paroxysm of pain.

'Oh God,' cried Bibi softly, again clinging to Haroon.

Rasoul bent down to his father, taking his hand. Looking up at Bibi he murmured, 'He dead.'

Haroon repeated the word, like a refrain. Outside, the wind kept hurling; thunder cracked and everyone started to run away from the bridge, the river, the spreadeagled tree – all except one or two of the youths who were eager to look at the old man's face. They asked Haroon, 'Is true de old man dead?' as if this was incredible.

The rain whipped against their faces. Haroon looked at Bibi in the moon's light, then at her father. Lightning streaked across the sky, lit up the fallen branches, the leaves of the once mammoth tree at their feet.

Bibi and Haroon stood alone now. From the window of the house, Rasoul watched them, and once more thought of his wife Shamoon, lovely, devoted... and of time passing by.

GO TELL CROSBIE

Pssst!

Sati hears this sound in the bound-coolie yard, the evening breeze blowing hard, frangipani and lotus blossoms mixed with cowdung rising in the air as she crinkles her nostrils. She's tired after a hard day's work in the creole gang.

Pssst!

No, she won't go.

Slim-waisted, with strong features and a straight nose, she often looks at herself in the mirror and knows how attractive she is. She knows that Overseer Simpson has had his eyes on her, often watching her wielding a cutlass in the field.

Pssst!

She's both flattered and frightened, for Overseer Simpson's a white man, a man with power. He'd said to her, when the other women in the weeding gang were out of earshot: 'Meet me, tonight; I'll come.'

'Come?' Her tone soft, she frowns.

'Yes.'

He speaks quickly, and she has difficulty understanding him, keeping up with his words. There's something gross and absurd about his large-bellied, pink-skinned presumption, the long whiskers he keeps twirling close to his ears. Yet there's a

brute strength in him which frightens her. Ha, no one refuses to
meet Overseer Simpson after work.

Pssst! Come and meet me, girl!

Sati knows that to go with Overseer Simpson would further
damage her reputation in the yard. They tease her endlessly
about her difference; she, who doesn't belong with anyone: a
dougla whom the Indians jeer at, and no respectable Indian man
would dream of marrying, though she looks more Indian than
African.

'No!' she wants to scream at Simpson who all the while
laughs. But what choice has she? There's Rudi, African like her
father, who likes her, but no more than that — though, when
there was talk of Simpson's interest in her in the yard, Rudi had
said, 'Dat man, you see, he go lead you to ruin.'

She'd sucked her teeth hard at him.

'You brazen, woman!'

'Ah mind me own business!' she'd snapped.

'He not like we.'

'I'm not like you — like none o' you!'

But Rudi had only joked: 'Ow Sati, you prappa lovely when
you angry, gal.'

'You always been sayin' dat. So why you not marry me?'

'How me gon marry you?'

'You can — if you want to.'

Their conversation is always like this. It seems to Sati that
nothing between them is ever serious. Yes, she has to be
married one day; to someone; to him? But Rudi? She likes him
more than she'll ever admit to him, but does he have any real
feelings for her? She feels the aches in her body after the day's
hard work, but she also feels stirrings of desire which frighten
her. Ah, what does it matter? What emptiness lies ahead?

II

Overseer Ron Simpson often wishes he were back in England, away from the blistering heat and humidity, but he's signed a contract, to serve 'King Sugar' as it's laughably called. His folks back in Liverpool are dirt-poor and he needs the money. At least the rum's cheap; the dark local brew dulls the emptiness of many mosquito-infested nights.

It's a lonely life; so few chances to meet the stuck-up white women who live in this godforsaken place. Yes, he knows a certain propriety has to be kept, a social code, because he's white; yet, for his sanity, he has to be free to come and go a little.

The stirrings of desire are impossible to deny, even though he feels a little guilty about Amelia back in England. She wants him to come back in a year's time, but there isn't much chance of that.

'I will marry you.'
'You won't, I know it.'
'Yes, by my honour.'
'Do you have any honour, Ron?'
'I swear it, Amelia.'
'Cross your heart, say you'll die — if you don't.'
'I'll die if I don't.' But he'd laughed, hard.
'But tell me you love me, Ron.'
'I love you, Amelia. Why don't you come with me to Guiana?'
'I can't, you know that.'
'What're you afraid of?'
'Malaria.'
'There's always quinine.'
'The heat, I hear...'
'Are you afraid of reptiles that run like strange dogs, zig-zag? Lizards, all prehistoric, that will swallow you with one bite!'
'No!'

'Then you'll come.'

'No, Ron.'

'Do you think I'll cross my heart and die?'

'Only if you find another woman — '

'There will be none like you, Amelia dear.'

'A pretty mulatto woman, maybe?'

'What do you know about that?'

'One of them was as black as the ground, the other white!'

'I will never love any one else, Amelia.'

'You will lie with her.'

'It's not the same.'

'You will climb between her thighs.'

'It's still not the same.'

'You will crawl inside her like a worm...'

'Then you must come...'

'You will die.'

'How so, Amelia?'

'At the hand of a slave...'

'There are no slaves left.'

'Then who are they?'

'Africans, Indians — they're all the same!'

'Still, I won't come.'

'I'll return, Amelia.'

'Cross your heart, Ron.'

III

In the dead hours of despair between work and sleep, Sati sits frozen in her distress. She who knows no other worlds, who feels the hard edges of other people's boundaries, the restless sensations of her spirit, she dreams of other places.

'Sati, you hear me, you too own-way, gal!'

'Wha', Ma.'

'You hard-ears, me say!'

'But Ma, is wha wraang me do?'

'Me say, gal, you is your own self now; you can no longer live wid we!'

'Wha' mek, Ma?'

'Is wha' you faader say.'

'Oh Gawd, Ma.'

'He say you have to go now, Sati.'

'Because of wha'?'

'Gal, you is a mixed-child, a strange pickney since the day you been baan!'

'No Ma, you not to say dat.'

'Yet me love you, child.'

'And Pa?'

'He gone away to canefield, then rice field — all day an' night.

'Ma, why you marry he?'

'Me love he.'

'You sure, Ma?'

'Yes, gal.'

'And you own ma an' pa, why they ask you to leave? Why they never want you to come back?'

'Cause you pa is African...'

'And you is Indian, right?

'Sati, dat is laang time ago.'

'Me feel sad, Ma.'

'Just like me and you pa. Is we lot!'

'Overseer Simpson, he go make it easy for me...'

'Gal, be careful wid dat Overseer Simpson.'

'Wha' you know bout he, Ma?'

'He one wicked-wicked man!'

'Is not true, eh?'

'Is wha' everyone say.'

'He promise to let me go home early, ever' day.'

'Sati, be careful. Me warn you!'

'Ma, he nice to me.'

'He just want to fasten heself betwen you legs — man always like dat.'

'Oh Gawd, no Ma!'

'That Overseer Simpson, me never really know 'bout he. But everybady talkin' now; so be careful.'

'Rudi tell me the same.'

'Ow Gawd, Rudi know too?'

'Yes... Ma.'

IV

The sharpness of the sun is like a knife, a sudden fierce pain. Rudi pulls down a fence, and builds it up again; his breathing harder; telling himself he must work longer each day and night; build a cow-pen for tomorrow's milk in this rain-splattered land; moaning, then laughing suddenly by himself as in a strange madness... Christ, Sati, is wha' wraang wid you, eh? Tell me who you really plan to marry? Sati, gal, you know I love you; you can't be worrying wid dat Overseer Simpson, eh. Is me, you own kind; never mind you mumma is an India bound-coolie, you daddy is an African like me; an' no matter if you mumma feel she disgrace she family. But is wha' we goin' to do? We's the same. Dougla, eh! In this backwater place, so far away from India or Africa, Christ! Come to you' senses, gal; dat wha' me a say...

In his broken potsherd of a house, the roof shingles flying about in the wind and rain, Rudi talks to himself in a strange madness, voices in his head. What future's in store for him? A jail term in faraway England? Would they parade him before a packed courthouse of white spectators, eager to see this novelty? Would they fasten a chain to his legs, hold him in a dungeon? Would there be trial by jury? Or would they just lynch him as in cotton plantation America? Maybe it would be better to avoid the threat from challenging Overseer Simpson.

Sati, you hear me?

Fear amidst the blacksage, jamoon, bougainvillea, water hyacinths. Fear amongst yams shooting up from the ground like miracles. Fear in the rice fields turned putrid from over cultivation. Fear amongst the sugar cane stalks which, bent by the wind, can't reach the sun and turn bitter, like gall.

Rudi mutters his rage.

Sati, keep away from Overseer Simpson; he na mean good, eh. He go lead you astray, he never go tek you back to England. He diff'ent from we; me done tell you; an' indenture-time not yet done, cause is more ship coming from India... And na think that because Commissioner-man Crosbie here from England, who looking after the welfare of all-we people, that you can do as you please. Mr Crosbie going to write fancy report, but you won't able fo' read it! Dat's all I say. Remember, gal, I gon marry you so we go live together as husband an' wife; and one day, we go have children; never mind they truly mix-up, and they ent know African or Indian language any longer but we own Dutch-English-African-Indian-mix-up talk, with its own grammar an' parts o' speech. An' let that one who call heself Fowler tek note, too, eh! Believe me, we taak got figure o' speech, intonation like music. So, Sati, come wid me before me go outa me mind. Me does think 'bout you at night, imaginin' you belly swell up wid white-man pickney, oh Gawd! Forget that maggot-skin Overseer Simpson man in the dark! He'll be gone in a couple o' months' time, back to his lily-white sweetheart, an' you gon never see he again. I know some of we people screamin' to go back to Africa and India; but it never going happen, cause now we bound to this Guiana mud-ground!

V

Darkness: a hen scratching feverishly in its coop; a raccoon making its deliberate way, following the scent in the air; someone coughing in a sudden fit; the hen waiting, turning-twisting, the other hens scratching frenziedly in the raftered darkness, feathers falling, piling on the grass, the blood-wet ground, where Sati, now awake, walks about in a white dress, hem pulled up, exposing her thigh. Overseer Simpson watches her with an unrelenting stare, burning to touch, caress, and overwhelm...

Pssst!

Is me, Sati? I am here.

You hear me, gal?

Amelia? Do you have eyes to see from afar?

Pssst!

All the indentured, all the enslaved, all you who have crossed the dreaded Middle Passage in the holds of ships... will you witness?

Sati makes her way slowly through the meandering brush. What did he promise her? Less work, more pay? A piecemeal bargain?

'Are you there, Sati?'

'Yes, me come.'

'Good, Sati'

'I'm afraid.'

'What for?'

'Me not know why?'

'Ha, don't be afraid. Remember who I am.'

'Yes, Overseer Simpson.'

'I am in perfect control.'

'Tell me you love me, na?'

'Love?'

Tremor of limbs; blacksage leaves shaking, rustling, overhearing; other tremors: trees; the hen coop's shiver; the lone raccoon making its way with orb-like eyes; turning, looking up. Despite the clouds' absence only a lone star's to be seen. A dog bays at the moon.

Simpson grabs hold of Sati's hand; pulls her to him, embracing her sinewy body, dragging her to the ground, to the mattress of leaves now quaking with his heave and thrust. Sati moans, pulling away. The raccoon closer, more deliberate than ever, follows the stronger scent, confused. Pulling Sati's face to his, Simpson crushes her lips; she claws in fury, wanting him and not wanting him because of who he is, maggot-white in the darkness.

Sati cries with pain, her harsh desire to be free for a moment from her prison of skin: Who is she? Who does she belong to?

Mr Crosbie, do you hear? Write that in your report.

'Please... Oh God, Overseer Simpson, leave me alone. I must hurry back!'

'Must? It's too late now, Sati.'

'I must go now.'

'No!'

'Let go of me!'

'You can go when I say so.'

'You're spent.'

'I am not. There's always more, you understand.'

'Let me go! Rudi!'

'Why do you cry for that nigger... Who's he anyway?'

'He gon marry me?'

'No one will. You'll be ready for me, each time I want you.'

'Oh God, no! Let me go... please.'

The brush disturbed, the ground shaken, tremors in each stone, grain of sand, and clod of clay; drops of water detach and fall from the trees.

Rudi, are you there?

A sharp cutlass raised in mid-air.

A white prick hanging loose.

Blade coming down.

Blood spurting.

Overseer Simpson, do you feel pain?

Rudi, what rage lurks in you? Your spirit and mind seething.

Sati running away.

'He dead! Oh Gawd!'

Sati's voice in the wilderness of the racing bush, leaves sprinting, stalks, branches falling quickly and surprising the ground. Blood still flowing; rivulets, streams: the creek's silent witness; a fish's testimony; what eyes could not see, yet observed by all the mute witnesses.

The racoon goes away now, its head lowered, the feathered ground footprinted with more blood.

A mourning, later.

Commissioner Crosbie's pen scratches the ground of parchment, dotting the i's, crossing the t's; a report to the British Parliament. But in what records can the feel of blood flowing be kept. Only words' silence.

Or mute rage.

A figure of speech in the sun, a tongue hanging out, dried-up, like skin on a barbed wire. Black or brown, a man's or woman's body, stretched out.

A MIGHTY VISION

'Dead, when you go leave here, man?' Again and again they called this out to him and laughed, as if to confirm they were bound to this place and the incessant whacking of cutlass against cane-stalk, which sometimes echoed in Dead's ears at night. Sometimes he even wondered if it was true, as he had read somewhere, that human beings evolved from sugar cane.

Suddenly he cried out, 'It's a damned lie!' and grunted in such a way that his entire body shook.

His mother frowned and looked at him curiously. Best to leave him to his ways, his mulling.

Dead was looking at a magazine: pictures of America which he'd been studying for days. He'd begun thinking recently that perhaps his dreams weren't unrealizable.

'Dead, you t'ink you can make it, man!'

'You really t'ink you can be a weightlifter?'

Mr Universe! He, a Charles Atlas or Joe Weider looking back from the magazine's pages. Yes, only five-foot six, skinny as he was, but strong, you better believe it, despite the paltry food, the flies hovering in Ramsingh's cakeshop where they often ended up after the long day in the canefield. Dead smiled, seeing himself transformed. Then he was thrashing through the canefield, muscles rippling in his back in the bright sunshine, tearing at the stalks, hurling bundle after bundle into the cane punt. Yes, he, Dead — and maybe no one would call him such a name again — a Tropical Mr Universe!

He started laughing hard; let them watch him good: Sumintra, Bibi, Devi, Sheena, and that mixed-race Potagee girl, Mabel. The sweat was pouring down his arms, neck, chest; he felt confident as never before, but then the thought raced though his mind that he shouldn't go back to the canefield; he'd tell the manager, tell him to his face, what he intended doing.

His mother, again watching him, smiled.

Not long after, in the bottom-house, Dead started lifting weights, intent on pressing two hundred pounds; then a straight clean-and-jerk... a real Charles Atlas. Maybe he'd need to pop those fancy steroid pills (where he'd get them from he didn't know), but he'd be the strongest, no matter what. He was making real progress, everyone applauding him as he lifted the weight again, a cleaner jerk this time.

'Man-Dead, you's de best!' said Shankar, hands to his waist, studying him more than the rest.

'Wha'?' Dead asked, breathing hard.

'You're the best, a real Mr Universe!'

Dead pressed his lips together doubtfully.

Shankar smiled, amazed at what he saw in Dead's eyes: as if those same eyes would pop out at him.

'You mean that?' Dead wiped another gob of sweat from his forehead. He was determined to free himself, but it began to feel too good to be true; it was happening so fast. Who was he to escape their fate, trapped on the sugar estate? He rubbed his eyes again, the magazine's pages before him. Charles Atlas and Joe Weider — the two strongest men in the world! And he'd be number three: his own picture on the magazine covers.

He saw his mother looking down at him from the landing above the bottom-house, listening to Shankar chaffing him about his not going back to the canefield. She was frowning.

Dead knew why. Their livelihood depended on his working in the fields; yet he kept imagining faraway places; seeing himself in an exhibition with some of the best weightlifters in the world. Again he started exercising, jerking the weights high, dumbells, barbells, his veins knotted; the pain immense. He strained all his muscles, every ounce of energy in him, and then, finally, he let out his breath in a whoosh.

'You did it, man,' cried Shankar. 'You did!'

He was in Madison Square Garden, New York; then, in London's Albert Hall. Mabel was there among the spectators; she'd come all the way here to watch him, cheer him on... unless, well, she'd emigrated, was now living in London. She'd come to see him, the Tropical Mr Universe, representing all of Guyana, Aruba, Jamaica, Trinidad, Barbados, Cuba! Her lips were mouthing mutely: YOU DID IT, DEAD! But what about Bibi, Rukmin, the others? Why weren't they also among the spectators?

Suddenly he felt his spirit sinking; he was sweating more than usual. What if he didn't make it? He dreaded going back to the canefield: to the soot, ash that stuck to his legs, navel, armpits, which he couldn't easily wash away no matter how hard he rubbed himself with Lifebuoy at the end of the day's work.

His mother said, 'Son, you okay?' He nodded to her. 'You sure?'

'Yes-yes,' he snapped, thoughts whirring, muscles tense, aching, as if his blood was leaking out of his body.

'Son... you arright?'

He tried to recall the applause: Ragubir, Anand, Mohan, Duleep, Simon; the girls too: Rohini, Sheena, Mabel — always the latter — all watching him, but he also heard Rohit's berating voice: 'You not like them American and British people, cause you got to cut de blasted cane. You can't be thinking 'bout being one o' the best in the world when you workin' so damned hard! You's a damn coolie like the rest o' we

— you baan here!' Then it was Mabel's laughter mocking him.

He looked at his mother, at her wrinkled face, long pendulous ears, eyes sunk in their sockets. She was muttering: 'Son, wha' get into you? Jombie-spirit?' Her eyes closed as if to shut out these spirits of the underworld — Indian and African combined, interchangeable, inexact — conjured up so easily in this moment of anxiety.

But he shook his head in denial, though when he concentrated hard the vision remained with him, so many nights wrapped together in this moment of dreaming, a sudden fulfillment of who he was and wanted to be.

Listening and not listening he heard her say, 'You go be okay, son; sleep well. You must keep up you' strength to cut cane again tomorrow.' Outside: the wind, a kitten yowling in the backyard, a dog howling, then an ass's deafening bray. Inside his mind's own darkness, like shutters against the moon's light: canefields again, the sound of the cutlass chopping.

Early the next morning he found himself in the canefield, working hard, bending and chopping cane. Kuldip said to him, 'Tek it easy, Dead-man. You got de whole day, eh.' But Dead only grunted, gripping the cutlass harder in the morning sun's already blazing heat; something inside him driving him along, goaded by each cane-stalk crashing before him. Simon, an African, stood back and watched with a sneer.

'You t'ink you go pump iron after this, Dead?' But there was a flicker of pain on Simon's face as he watched Dead wipe his neck where it itched because of the sticky soot and sweat gathered there, his mouth set hard as he continued chopping.

Now it was Sharab's turn to jeer as Dead started gathering the stalks of cane into a bundle, hauling it on his narrow shoulder, carrying it to the punt and throwing it in with a loud clang. Dead, as they all knew, was in a hurry to get home to further his ambitions.

'Dead-boy, you goin' to make the white people rich if you cut cane so fast,' Sharab said. Simon added: 'Maybe they'll take you to Cuba, Jamaica, Aruba, even to blasted India and Africa, so you can show black people everywhere how to cut cane, eh!'

But Dead shut out the voices; and so neatly, so almost without resistance did his machete — which he'd spent long hours sharpening — slice through the cane stalks that he was amazed at his own dexterity. Maybe he'd have enough energy left to pump iron that afternoon: his steadfast, determined bench-press — the weight in the air, all two hundred pounds of it! But then he shuddered at the image of the weight falling on him, his head crushed to a pulp. 'You're the best!' he heard Simon say. Did he mean the best cane-cutter?

Dead's thoughts went back to Mabel, not to Rohini or Devi — they were always so shy and demure. Was it Mabel's outgoing, 'wayward' ways he found so attractive, or was it because she was of mixed race — African, Portuguese and something else — that she excited him. He knew his mother wanted him to marry an Indian girl when that time came. 'Son, you mus' settle down wid we own kind,' she'd said. Once more he chopped at the cane, thinking vaguely of the faraway places he'd visit as the Tropical Mr Universe. Then, maybe, he'd talk about cane-cutting being the blasted hardest work in the world! Let those who think they were strong, who grew up on Cadbury's milk chocolate and ate porridge for breakfast, imagine they could do this work in the sun's fierce heat. He wiped more perspiration from his face, and lashed out at the cane with his machete gripped firmly in his hand.

'Take it easy, Dead. Is already past eleven o'clock; you can't cut cane like this all day, or else you go fall down and be really... dead!'

Dead sighed as he looked at Shankar's scowling face. Next he looked up at the cirrus clouds moving slowly against the sky's aquamarine-blueness-turned-blotched whiteness. Again a passing vision of being elsewhere: Mabel was with him. Devi and Rohini — let them follow him too, all admiring the shape of his well-muscled body in a few months' time. He heard Mabel still laughing hard among the spectators; then his mother's words, repeated like a mantra: 'Son, we's Indian, eh.' She smiled, cajoled. 'You fader shoulda see you now.' Would he, he who had died suddenly of a stroke more than five years ago?

Dead quickly threw another bundle of cane into the now almost full iron-punt. As he turned, Simon, just behind him, nearly tumbled forward. Dead made a quick move to help him and suddenly he felt a strange pain in his stomach... Christ, this wasn't real, was it? Maybe he was hungry, or he needed something to drink. 'Dead, you okay?' two or three others asked at once when they saw his pale expression, contorted face; how he almost buckled, couldn't stand up straight.

'Take it easy, man; it hotter today,' another urged. 'Besides you can't be cutting too much cane and be pumping iron like you do all last evening.'

Dead forced a smile, waving them off. 'Son, take it easy,' his mother's voice, somewhere in his mind; and Mabel still laughing: 'Come on, Dead, you love me, true-true? You sure you'll take me to Aruba and Cuba? Africa too? Ha, I'll do things with you that no shame-faced Hindu woman would, eh.' Mabel's loud laughter, her attractive body, all curves; the fullness of her mouth: all this he wanted to experience. 'Dead, you sure you okay?' Shankar enquired, as Dead once more felt the sharp pain on the right side of his stomach. What was it? Maybe he'd leave now, he'd done enough of this piece-work. He'd start off on the four miles walk for home. Then, maybe, he'd still lift weights that afternoon.

'Go on, Dead-man, go an' rest,' said Simon, holding up his machete against the sun's glare.

They watched him walk away, he who'd never been absent from work before. Why they called him Dead, they didn't really know; maybe it stemmed from a vague remark about his desire to live a long life right after his father's sudden death. Whatever, it had quickly turned into one of the many nicknames that floated around — ribald, banal and sometimes excruciatingly cruel: names such as Shanks, Lame-foot, Fatso, Bald-Head. As they watched him, they wanted to call out to him to walk slower, then faster, because he seemed to be hurrying home, then dawdling. They couldn't be sure.

Dead stayed in his room flipping through the pages of the magazines, figuring that no one fully understood his dreams: not his mother, nor Mabel. He smiled to himself, then sighed heavily.

'You sure you okay, son?' his mother asked, appearing again at the door.

He looked at her, the magazine held tightly in his hand, thinking that all one had to do was set one's mind to it. There was no way he wanted to return to the canefield. No! He must, above all else, continue to pump iron in order to be the best. The pain, whatever it was, seemed to be no more. He smiled.

'Bhai, you must go back to work tomorrow, eh,' his mother coaxed, with a mild impatience.

Suddenly Dead started putting on his clothes, though he was not sure what he intended doing. But make no mistake, in his red tie, navy-blue jacket, he looked handsome! What do you think Mabel?

'Bhai, how you dress up like dat — like film-star, eh? You t'ink you na go cut cane anymore? Why you na wear backdam clothes?' Puzzlement, anxiety, rebuke flitted through the words.

Dead was exhilarated as he stepped out. A few villagers on the main road watched him, astonished. Was that really Dead, one of their own, who now looked taller, like a stranger among them? Mabel, Dularie, Rukmin, you should see him now! What was he up to, where was he going? To London? New York?

Again the impulse to jeer as they watched him taking long strides, head in the air, cocky, arrogant; no longer the common cane-cutter.

Dead was heading for the senior management compound, to tell them who he was, what he wanted to do. He felt his muscles taut, bulging under his sleeves, but the white-starched shirt made his skin itch a little in the sun's heat and the jacket he wore was suddenly oppressive. Yet he stepped on faster, breathing in the slight wind blowing from the coast. Was that pain in his stomach still there? He pictured the compound ahead with its well-manicured lawns, where the overseers and managers lived — all from abroad, no?

'Bhai, you sure you know wha' you doin'?' his mother's soft rebuke hung in the wind. What was he doing? He should turn back now, at once. He heard the factory's grinding noise, steam pouring out as far as he could see, rising up to join the clouds. It was so overwhelming. What was he doing here? Yet he stepped on.

He breathed in, sighed, sucked in more air. His legs wobbled, weakening, but the canefield's scorching heat in his mind's eye pushed him on. He reached the main door. Now, he was suddenly furtive, unsure. He looked in. Sitting there was this attractive girl, lipstick, rouge, silk blouse: so confident. A secretary or administrative assistant, maybe; fairskinned, from the town, no doubt. Typewriter before her, she glanced at him, frowned. Who was he?

He dithered.

She looked at him from the corners of her eyes.

'I come...'

'What?'

'I come to see de manager.'

'You have an appointment?'

'No... er... I...'

'You must have an appoint...'

'I must just see him.' He'd rehearsed what he wanted to say.

But she kept looking at him: Are you sure? Who are you anyway, dressed up like that? You can't hide the fact you're just a coolie cane-cutter. Dead saw all this, but he gritted his teeth, refused to budge; he must see the MANAGER! He was losing his patience, he said.

She half got up, about to show him out. But maybe she'd let him wait a while. Maybe wait all day; when he was tired, he'd leave. But Dead stood his ground, raising his voice; jacket, shirt-collar itching in the air-conditioned office.

A tall man, cool, suave, stepped out from the main office door. He looked hard at Dead, frowned. Dead retreated a few inches, though he offered an awkward smile.

'What do you want?'

Dead mumbled. He wanted to shed this false skin of clothes, piece by piece, jacket first, then tie. He wanted to be back in the canefield with Sharab, Ragubir, Simon; wanted to be amongst the smell of raw sugar cane, burnt leaves, soot, dead insects, animals, that acrid smell always in the air; to feel the solid weight of a bundle of cane bearing down on his shoulder... Yet here he was in this clean office with fancy upholstery, facing the manager! And he must tell him how hard cane-cutting was, how he hated it, who he was and what he wanted to be...

'I come... for a...' he stammered.

'A what?'

'A job... You see, I work in the canefield.'

The manager wasn't sure he was hearing correctly. A smile flitted at the corners of his mouth because he felt he was looking at a comedian: there were all sorts who lived in this mixed-up place where all kinds of madness and eccentricity flourished.

'You see, er... I want a job in the office,' Dead ventured, looking at the man's high forehead.

'Office?'

Silence.

'Yes — right here,' Dead blurted out, unable to keep his thoughts bottled up any longer. 'You see, I'm the best cane-cutter, honest to God. But I come here 'cause I want an office job. Yes, something easy now, 'cause I need lighter work.' Dead felt as if it wasn't he who was saying these words as he looked at this tall man before him, who was so much in command of his environment. Yet Dead wanted to tell him more, about his lifting weights and one day becoming the Tropical Mr Universe. Yes, he — five-foot-six Sooklall — his real name; not Dead anymore. He, the best damned cane-cutter around, who kept pumping iron after work each day; yes, he needed an easy job to give him energy left to fulfill his ambition. Mabel, do you hear?

The best damned clean-an'-jerk he'd make! Yes, Mr Ross, look at me good. My muscles, well-defined, the best yet! You could come and see me at Madison Square Garden in New York, or at the Royal Albert Hall in London; or at the Skydome in Toronto, no? Mabel, are you still with me? Dead wasn't sure of what was he was saying or only thinking: the words just kept coming out in a torrent.

'I don't mean any rudeness by comin' here... see... I mean,' he added, 'dressed up like this, though I am a cane-cutter...'

The fan whirred; the air was cool in the office, but Dead suddenly started feeling the heat, the manager's glare, the sniggering of the rouged, lipsticked girl in the background.

'What you say your name is?'

His name? Not Dead... No! Or, maybe that! Yes, tell him his name was Dead!

Mr Ross loomed taller. Dead began shrinking; he couldn't stand there much longer. The walls were closing in on him and he yearned for the open canefield, the hot air, soot on his face, cane leaves bruising his arms and legs; even that pain in his stomach.

The manager suddenly started laughing, head tilted back, mouth widening, looking at the ceiling and laughing so hard that the whole building seemed to resound. Dead saw his dreams crashing down before him: a Mr Universe crumbling, body frail, weak; and he felt the tremor of his former pains all over him, and anger throbbing in his head. He suddenly gripped the chair near him, until he could feel it breaking in his hands; the manager was still laughing, his mouth lop-sided, his dignity gone.

'You... you want an office job, eh, Mr, er... Dead. You, ha-ha. Cane-cutter, you think... ha!'

'I am... the BEST.'

Dead was thinking of his dream, which wasn't like a dream anymore, but something else. Next he was grabbing at this collar-and-tie man whose skin was pale, shaking him so hard his eyes almost started popping out. No... no; this wasn't happpening; nothing was real any longer.

Right after, he started walking out, the girl sniggering loudly, Mr Ross staring after him. Dead was glad he was leaving, his muscles rippling under his shirt, a Charles Atlas-Tropical Mr Universe. He felt good for having come here to present his case, really good. As he walked, he felt the ground under his feet was sacred, though his steps were awkward. In this very place, the soil where the crops were planted, where green leaves sprouted and waved in the wind: all this was in him now, singing his broken dreams. Did they matter any more? Maybe Mr Ross was still standing there at the window trying to figure out who he really was, red tie and all. Ah, was he a party worker? One of them!

Dead walked faster in the fullness of the sun's heat; and *he* didn't mind it, didn't need the fan to cool the air; he only breathed it heavily and felt stronger and walked faster. In the background, the factory hummed; all of England, America, Canada, the whole world throbbing, a mammoth hum as he kept walking on. It was all because of the cane he'd cut. Yes, he was telling everyone that: who he was, what he intended doing, right there at Madison Square Garden, Royal Albert Hall, Toronto's Skydome. The crowd was before his mind's eye, applauding him: Mabel, Rohini, Devi; his mother too. And Mr Ross and that girl were still looking out of the window in astonishment. Dead walked faster, feeling the full weight and style of his jacket, head held high like a pillar to the clouds...

'Who you been to see, Dead? Mr Ross himself, eh?'

Disbelief in the air.

'And wha' you tell he?'

'Wha', eh?'

'He chase you out, Dead? Tell we!'

But Dead wasn't listening to them, only smiling, feeling the sun on his neck and the scarce breeze. His mother muttered, 'Son, is good you come home. You fader would a be really proud o' you, so well you look!' She studied him, head to toe, appraising him as if he was no longer her son. 'An' who you been to see, eh? Is true wha' everyone say, that is the big-boss Mr Ross himself you meet?'

Dead walked past her and, picking up the magazine once more, he looked at the face of this Mr Charles Atlas and he wondered if this white man could cut cane like he did? Could he really face the sun's heat, feel the sting of soot in his eyes, and the burning of raw sweat mixed with ash on his neck, arms, chest, with scores of insects flitting by. Could he really?

No, only he! Dead began laughing hard, the more he looked at this Mr Charles Atlas-Joe Weider. Yes, only he... and Baldeo, Ragubir, Simon, and the others. Laughing harder, he was telling Mr Ross this too, and that girl in the office with its air-conditioned atmosphere and fancy upholstery. He went to the bottom-house, and at once started lifting weights, the clean-and-jerk — two hundred and fifteen pounds, the heaviest ever! It felt so good. All this was in preparation for his return to work early the next morning when he'd cut the cane faster than anyone;

and maybe one day he'd indeed go to America, Europe, Canada
— not to Africa, Asia, the Philippines — to demonstrate his
quickness, strength... who he really was. Let the world know
that! His ma was still close by, muttering: 'Bhai, me really been
worry 'bout you.' Smiling, proud of him and again talking about
his father: who he was; repeating his name like a rhapsody.
Dead heard the trees, the soil, the sun and the rain singing.

LOSERS

The rope stiffened in his hand as the young bull veered to the right, then just as suddenly veered to the left. Snakie's wrist, bruised bluish-black, burned from the pain. The rope felt like an extension of himself. The animal pulled again, frantically charging, and Snakie braced himself hard against the ground, heels dug in, though just as quickly he stepped forward in a short run to keep pace with the animal. He swore, spitting out a jet of saliva that sizzled on the asphalted road. His bare feet were now blistered, large toes spread out unnaturally as he struggled on. The road ahead shimmered, the heat's consistency like a sheet of rain.

Fatigue was beginning to take its toll as he saw his shadow grow larger, and then, almost instantaneously, shrink. He grimaced, his wrist burning, the animal snorting, sniffing, wayward as ever. He had been two hours at it, and his throat was parched. He'd stopped a few miles back to quench his thirst, but his throat again itched unbearably; the desire to drink something stronger than water gnawed at him. He swallowed, his throat a bunched knot; he felt gripped by the wild urge to drink himself into a state of abject stupor.

'Gwan!' he barked at the bull; the words slurred, his tongue heavy.

'Gwan!' he barked again. Suddenly it was as if the animal

heard him, for it pricked up its ears and turned around and faced him, their eyes almost level: as if the beast was expressing a strange familiarity with him. To whom did the bull really belong? Snakie looked at it long and hard. More softly now, he urged it on, the bull moving, cantering.

Snakie trotted behind, smiling, because he was being obeyed. But he stopped, spat and wiped away a bead of sweat hanging on his brow when again he started thinking about Sergeant Dumphries. It was Dumphries with whom he'd have to bargain for payment when he handed over the catch. 'Stray-catcher,' Dumphries called him sneeringly, then always laughed loudly.

The reddish-grey police station loomed ahead, and a tremor went through Snakie's veins. 'Gwan!' he let out, hoarsely. The bull snorted, kicked up dirt. 'Gwan-Gwan!' he barked, straining every ounce of energy left in him. A cluster of bystanders, youths mostly, unemployed idlers, gathered around to heckle.

'Snakie-man, you can't take dat bull to the 'pound!'

'Stray-catcher, leave de blasted animal alone!' another hollered.

'Sergeant Dumphries en' goin' pay you anyt'ing!' a one-eyed youth taunted.

Snakie cringed, wished he was doing some other work, though he figured he had no choice really. He spat in disgust, the heat growing suddenly more intense. Would the sergeant cheat him? Offer him only a few paltry dollars, without acknowledging the difficulty of his work?

'Don't forget he's a blackman, he en like we,' another called.

Snakie's throat felt more parched; the ground beat in waves under his feet.

'Why you don't find work on the estate, Snakie-man!' the one-eyed youth yelled.

Snakie knew very well why he didn't. He had some independence as a stray-catcher: he could work as he pleased; he wasn't laid off when the crop season was over like the heckling youths; he didn't have to crawl to the overseers; and he also knew cane: the thud-thud of cutlass against cane stem, black ash from the burnt cane ridged on your face; the acrid smell of a canefield fire deep in your nostrils. But there was Dumphries! The rope twisted into a thick unruly knot at his wrist, the blood pumping through his veins in spasmodic beats. Again, his throat burned: he needed a drink.

No, he'd remain a stray-catcher, Dumphries or not. Suddenly the bull ran forward, tugging harder. Sweat leaked down his face. His heart pumped faster.

'Snakie-man, dat Dumphries goin' to suck you blood dry!'

This time Snakie felt he couldn't control the bull any longer, but it stopped running and stood firmly in one spot. The ground itself seemed to come to a standstill, each pebble, stone, brick, pulled together into a mound. Then the animal slowly turned. Snakie wasn't sure if he was actually here, or somewhere else; the faces of his wife and child appeared before him, then as suddenly disappeared.

The bull snorted, tail lifted high up.

A dust cloud rose from the ground under its hooves once more.

Dumphries folded and unfolded his arms with a suave, detached air. Snakie wished he was somewhere else. Dumphries, a black man from the town who'd come here to lord it over him, was, as ever, dressed to perfection. Dwarfed by his muscular frame, Snakie felt ragged and vulnerably small.

He wanted to hand over his catch quickly, take his paltry payment and be gone.

But Dumphries also challenged something he had to defend, as he heard again his baby crying and his wife's parting words to him as he left.

'Hope you en expectin' we to pay you for this,' Dumphries said, bringing Snakie's thoughts back to the present.

'You got to, Sergeant-er-Dum-phries,' Snakie faltered, turn-ing to look at the bull tied a few yards away from him, where it kicked the hard ground and snorted.

Dumphries smiled, folded his arms and looked down on Snakie with a mocking smile. Snakie put his hand to his throat as he remembered the winding road he'd just walked: the haze, heat, pebbles, stones, bricks, the bull's red eyes imprinted on his mind. Suddenly he wanted to take the animal back, hand it to its real owner. Maybe he should be working in the cane fields — not catching strays. Once again he thought of Parbattie — young, pretty, slim-waisted, desired, he knew, by a number of men. He felt the throb of his wrist, glanced at the broken capillaries.

Dumphries was standing like a man with all the time in the world.

Stray-catcher! Snakie heard Parbattie's taunts again. 'Maybe you go catch a tiger one day!' Last night she'd spurned his advances when he touched her, the curve of her waist, her thigh, challenging his manhood. She had rolled away to the far side of the bed and he was left there, erect and frustrated. A tiger or jaguar? How much would Dumphries pay then? Yes, a really ferocious beast, a killer of many cattle. If such an animal could be caught! It twisted and turned in his mind, a jaguar as high as a horse... he was roping it, pulling with all his might, the beast snarling, claws trying to tear chunks of flesh out of him, the jaws wide open... Aaaaaghh! His child's head was locked in them, about to be swallowed into that cavernous mouth! Parbattie was screaming, but oddly, as if she was also laughing.

Dumphries was laughing too.

Somewhere, a low growl.

He looked at Dumphries, the town-dweller; his presence here in the village an intrusion. Parbattie was saying, 'Is wha' you always think about, man?' and laughing after one attempt at love-making had ended in feeble failure, challenging him,

'Come on, man, ride me again, na?', arching her back at him, the jaguar itself!

Dumphries reeked of a heady cologne; so unlike the smell of cow's urine and stale sweat that clung to Snakie after his long day's work. Parbattie often rebuked, 'Why you na wash properly before you come to bed!'

Dumphries, Snakie had heard, was a womanizer, with a special taste for Indian women, their long straight hair and supple brown bodies. This thought became unbearable, and he spat hard a few feet from Dumphries's boots — a thin film of dust rising, then slowly trickling, disappearing.

'If you keep bringing these so-called strays, you will run the farmers out of business,' Dumphries said.

'Them destroy other people's property,' Snakie fired back, fingers to his throat, eyes bloodshot.

'Ah yes,' chuckled Dumphries, humouring him. 'But you must watch out!'

'Eh?'

'T'iefing farmer cow could get you killed.'

'Killed?'

'You wouldn't want that pretty wife of yours to lose her man.'

Right then Snakie wanted to tell the sergeant about bringing a jaguar to the compound. He'd drag it all the way from the heartlands and thrust it in front of him. Let all the villagers come to see this thing!

Dumphries kept on smiling, noting how shaken Snakie was. Maybe it was the fear of a threat to his life. Maybe the fool suspected something.

Now Snakie wanted to get home to his wife at once. The more he looked at the sergeant, the more conscious he was of his own rags, clothes smelling of cow's urine, wet rope. He had never felt so insecure before. He gritted his teeth, thinking that instead of Dumphries giving him money, he was throwing death in his face. Who'd want to kill him?

'Let them try.'

'Them?' Dumphries asked in a mocking tone.

'Those who want to... kill... me!' Snakie fidgeted, studying Dumphries' smiling face; and all the festering memory of strife between the races, Africans and Indians, burst like a boil. He hissed, 'Yes, let them try to kill me!' His lips twitched, jaw elongated. But the image of who his enemy might be shifted disturbingly. Could it be one of his own kind? In the background the bull mooed impatiently. Dumphries laughing; Parbattie scolding; the baby crying; a jaguar's growl. Snakie again looked at his wrist, bruised blood vessels, torn skin.

'Ten bucks is all you gon get today, Snakie.'

'Ten... only?' Snakie's heart pumped a fast beat.

'You think I have money to give away?'

Snakie felt the back of his neck itching. He stammered, 'You have to pay me more!'

Dumphries growled. 'More?'

They haggled, Dumphries increasingly getting the upper hand.

Snakie squirmed. Then another four dollars was handed to him: this only because of his generosity, Dumphries said.

A vague smile flitted across Snakie's mouth, near which a housefly hovered, ready to alight. Above the police compound, a lone carrion crow circled. Snakie looked up at it in a slant of sun, his eyes dazzled as he studied the crow's shadow, arabesque of wings against the shimmering haze from the zinc sheets roofing the houses. Then, on an impulse, he asked the sergeant how much he would pay for a jaguar.

Dumphries frowned. 'A jaguar?'

'A beast — which sneak around and kill cattle!' The words came in a tight, nervous rush.

'Oh?' Dumphries stretched out a hand and rested it on Snakie's shoulder.

Snakie studied the smooth hand, manicured nails: even as

he thought of the jaguar, his wife's words, the threats of death, the beast clawing, snarling, as he dragged it to the compound.

Dumphries hand dropped from Snakie's shoulder. 'A jaguar's not a stray.'

'How much you go pay me for it?' Snakie persisted.

The sergeant once more smiled and Snakie wondered if he'd pay fifty dollars! What, though, would Dumphries do with such a beast? He smiled, as the thought made him feel free, as never before, and he imagined his wife welcoming him home, his child giggling.

The villagers' eyes were on him as he walked home, the heavy rope coiled as always around his waist. When he'd had his drink, at first Snakie felt better. Now his head was filled with a confusion of voices: the idling youths taunting; the cries of jaguars and baboons, from the hinterland. He was bringing them to Dumphries one by one in growling frenzy, demanding each time, 'How much will you pay me?' Parbattie was there too, insisting on meeting Dumphries: he with his heady cologne. Each time the Sergeant was laughing harder.

'Dumphries, you should get the blasted hell outa here. You don't belong here!' he was saying.

'Dumphries pay you well, Dumphries pay you well?' the voices mocked like the heat's heavy tongue.

Now he was telling them that Dumphries was paying him more and more for each animal. There was no need to haggle any longer.

'Snakie, you been drinking too much!' another cried. 'Why you always walking with that heavy rope round you' waist?'

But Snakie was too dazed to think clearly anymore, and he didn't want to go home to his wife in this state. In his mind's eye he saw that self-same carrion crow in the air, wings flapping, the sun's somersault as the bird swooped down on him at that moment. Ah, they were really going to kill him! Was Dumphries leading him to the slaughter, a noose around his neck like a straying cow?

Snakie growled in his drunken state. The crow's eyes, the bird dropping from the sky; the jaguar leaping in the air; a horned bull charging him! Dumphries was laughing all the while; Parbattie beside him laughing too.

He was face-to-face to with Dumphries once more.

'What you here for?' Dumphries growled, though he no longer had his arms folded in casual confidence; he seemed tight, stiff, because something about the look in Snakie's eyes was odd this time.

'More payment — what else?'

'You crazy!' he snapped. 'Snakie, you been drinking too much; you can be locked up.'

'You cyan lock me up.' Snakie was focussing hard, trying to control his senses. 'Because, I'm a free man! And you a blasted blackman and I... an Indian.'

'Eh?' Dumphries was taken by surprise, but he quickly let out a short laugh.

'You na belong here!'

'Watch you lip. I'm here to enforce the law.'

Snakie sneered. 'A beast's law?'

The two men looked at each other with centuries of pain and rage.

'Snakie, go home to you pretty wife. Maybe you should watch out for straying animals nearer home.'

Snakie lunged forward at Dumphries who pushed him heavily in the chest. Snakie went sprawling in the dust.

'Snakie, go away before I plant my boot on your backside and lock you up. Leave here now before something bad happen to you!'

'You cyan kill me!' Snakie quickly answered. 'You not fit to be the law.' He picked himself up from the dust and said, to Dumphries' surprise, 'You got to promise to leave my wife alone.'

'Eh?'

Snakie moved closer to him, but then stood stock still, swaying unsteadily.

There was a clamour of jeering voices coming towards him. Had they come to kill him? At the head of the crowd was Parbattie. Were they going to kill Dumphries as well? At once the sergeant went down on all fours: half-man, half-beast! He was prancing around, snorting and pawing the ground, just out of reach.

Everywhere, a dozen Dumphries, moving around him, with horns, long ears, spotted skin. Snakie wiped away more sweat as if he was still in the sun's glare. What was real? The heavy rope around his waist, the distinct smell of the bull: urine, wet rope; pebbles, soil.

The crowd were laughing, then slowly they began to retreat in the shimmering haze.

He was not really aware that Dumphries had grasped his shoulder and was pushing him towards a cell.

From his cell window Snakie looked out and saw the carrion crow swooping down again; coming closer to his window, eyes really large. After a while there was no other sound, everyone was gone. How long had he been there? Where was Dumphries now? His wife? He couldn't hear his child's cry.

Slowly Snakie took the rope from round his waist and threw it up over a beam in the ceiling. His last thought was to wait until Dumphries appeared again, on all fours, to show him that it was the mark of a free man to be able to choose the moment of his end.

THE ALBINO

Mr Ben-Jamel once again considered his political prospects
and muttered the word 'people' with a strange sense of foreboding. Maybe he was just getting older. Once they had all opposed
the British, now it was: 'It's your kind causing all the problems... They should never have brought you people here.' Mr
Ben-Jamel shuddered. Yes, Indians hated Africans, and vice
versa. Now that the elections were once more drawing close, the
ill-feeling between the races came to the surface and seethed.

Ben-Jamel sighed. They did things better in America, Britain, even France. He often read the *Guardian*, *The Washington
Post*, *Le Monde*, sent to him by relatives or friends abroad. He
read out their editorials loudly as he sat in his club and gulped
down good whisky. At such times he was inclined to agree that
the upcoming elections were an unwanted nuisance — let the
races quarrel as much as they wanted — but then thought better
of it and wagged his *Times* in front of everyone. It wasn't only
the British who should have their justice, their Magna Carta; or
the Americans their long-standing belief in the Rights of Man;
these principles should be theirs too. Perspiration leaked down
his neck, as he made his point. The sad truth was, though, that
Indians voted for Indians, and Africans for Africans; it was just
a matter of making sure you got out your vote.

His friend, a high court judge, asked, 'What about the vote in your district? You're worried — you can't fool us!'

Ben-Jamel looked at his empty glass, frowned, then rasped, 'If we ran a cow, it wouldn't matter,' though truly he wanted people to vote according to what they thought was right.

'Then run an animal,' someone else quipped.

'But what stripes would this animal have?' Ben-Jamel asked the judge, an African, a suave, fastidious man who'd been trained at the Inns of Court in London.

More jousting, downing of whiskies. A Hindu lawyer versed in Sanskrit muttered sadly, 'It's our lot, of course, our uneducated lower class being so far away from the supports of their ancestral civilisation.'

The judge, a Christian of deep convictions, murmured wistfully, 'We were torn from Africa's pristine innocence.' He paused, then added hastily: 'Now Christ's love prevails amongst our people.'

'Indians had the first civilisation.'

'Not the Greeks?'

The discussion took off into flights of speculation, ranging wide over the world, fired by shots of whisky and Demerara rum. For a while Ben-Jamel and the high court judge heard only the enthusiasms of each other's mind.

'Sloth will destroy this nation,' Ben-Jamel finally said, as his energy ran down, clutching *The Times* and comparing the whiteness of its paper and its crisply printed columns with the inky, gremlin-smudged newspapers of his own country.

But then an idea gripped him. At once he hurried to the Leader of the Party — the idea growing in his mind.

'I have a solution,' he said, thrusting his hands into the air.

'Solution?' the Leader asked. 'To what?'

'To the racial conflict dividing our people.'

The Leader laughed, then muttered, 'You do? Old as you are...' and was going to add, 'and feeble-witted?'

Ben-Jamel had taken countless political knocks over the years; he wasn't fazed.

'Run an albino!' he said.

The Leader looked solemnly at him. 'Is that all?'

'It'll work!' Ben-Jamel surprised the Leader with his conviction. 'He will be of neither race.'

'An albino, eh? But will the people go for it?' Then the Leader became affable as he began to wonder whether there might be something in the idea. He wiped his thick horn-rimmed glasses, muttering, 'This problem certainly plagues our country, and much of the Third World.'

Ben-Jamel nodded. 'There are African albinos, Indian albinos, European albinos: no race would be able to claim such a person as their own.'

'Of course.' The Leader looked hard at Ben-Jamel. 'But you must remember, Ben-Jamel, we're a black race, we take pride in being black.'

'And brown..?'

The Leader looked impassively at Ben-Jamel. He figured he'd underestimated him all along.

'Well, why not somebody who is mixed African and Indian?'

'You know what the Hindi meaning of 'dougla' is?

'Point taken,' said the Leader.

'Of course, it might just be seen as a joke,' Ben-Jamel mumbled. 'You'd have to discuss the idea with the inner circle of the Party.'

'About the joke?' The Leader raised an eyebrow.

But Ben-Jamel was not to be put off and began thinking about where they might actually find such a man, an albino who'd have the interests of the party at heart: not to mention the district.

But where to find such a man? When it came to the point, Ben-Jamel couldn't recall ever having met an albino in his district, certainly not among the fisherfolk, labourers, rice farmers or sugar cane workers. There was one Amerindian tribe living deep in the interior who, people said, were as light-skinned as Europeans, but that was not the same thing at all.

Before long, word reached the various districts that the Party was working on a plan to end the country's racial problems, though how was a closely guarded secret. Among the inner Cabinet members mention of the albino idea aroused derisive laughter. The Leader was hearty about it; what the country needed was ONE UNDISPUTED LEADER (himself). After they'd won, he'd dispense with elections altogether in the tradition of a one-party state; the country wasn't ready yet for a multi-party system. Let the bigger powers without their racial problems wrestle with elections every four or five years: all that waste of time, energy, resources!

But among the country people, the idea of racial peace stirred imaginations.

'Now God would indeed be with us,' a rice farmer said as word of 'the plan' reached him. And another: 'All along we have been worshipping the one god with different names: Jesus, Allah, Krishna.' Hands were clasped; smiles floated about.

In the club, Ben-Jamel read the *Times*, smiling.

II

Mr Ferrar seemed to have been spirited out from nowhere; skin devoid of any colour, pasty-looking, a real albino, though previously no one had seen him as such. He had careful elocution, gestured modestly and was not given to facile bonhomie. He smiled only a little, but sincerely. People were inclined to see in him the absence of many colours or none.

As Ben-Jamel heard these reports he was intrigued. But he began to wonder when he met Ferrar, and the latter said to him, 'I've always had a political ambition, Mr Ben-Jamel. I'm looking forward to the day when I'll be in Parliament.' Was his idea such a good one after all? Was there a danger that Ferrar's popularity could outstrip his own? Nevertheless, he muttered encouragement: if Ferrar was to succeed it would be as his protégé.

But Ferrar, his would-be patron found, was disturbingly independent. He was drawn to politics, he said, out of genuine civic interest. There was so much to do. 'The primitiveness here...' and he looked at Ben-Jamel very squarely when he added, 'The lack of ideas, intellectual stimulation for the people.'

Ben-Jamel knitted his eyebrows; Ferrar was a plain speaker: would he make a good politician?

It was this, he told Ben-Jamel, which allowed race to dominate everything.

Ben-Jamel had to agree, but he looked at Ferrar closely — wondering which of the country's racial groups he really belonged to.

'I believe we have to develop a politics based on principles, Mr Ben-Jamel.'

'Here in the tropics?'

'We all need sound principles.'

'My dear fellow, I agree. But...' Ben-Jamel wasn't sure how to continue.

The two men smiled; there was an understanding of sorts. Ben-Jamel added that a man of principles would do well to bring this country into the twenty-first century. Just then he wanted to touch Ferrar, feel his skin, to see if it was indeed like paste.

As if Ferrar knew what the other was thinking, he laughed hard, but then said seriously, 'With the elections drawing near, it's time to get to work. I must meet the people who will vote for me.'

'I will take you around — introduce you.'

'Can't I just start campaigning on my own, Mr Ben-Jamel?'

Ben-Jamel pressed his lapels and smiled indulgently at Ferrar's naiveté.

Ferrar appeared not to notice and said, 'You understand, I must gain their confidence. Distrust is one of the easiest emotions to cultivate.'

Ben-Jamel nodded solemnly.

'You see this place has a history of politicians talking about exploitation, but themselves exploiting the people.'

'Exploitation?' Ben-Jamel's ears perked up. This at least was familiar party talk, but where was Ferrar coming from?

'For instance, all this talk of socialism. What good does it do the people? Where's the food in their bellies? What do you think, Mr Ben-Jamel? What do you really think?'

Ben-Jamel felt cornered: Ferrar was deliberately putting him on the spot. The Leader was an avowed socialist; Party discipline was necessary, and here was Ferrar starting to challenge the basic concept of the Party. Ah, yes, he wanted to tell him that over the years he'd had his disagreements with the Leader about socialism, Marxist-Leninism, democratic centralism and the many forms often discussed at Cabinet meetings: Russian, Chinese, Cuban; each a better scientific model. He had never really accepted the argument put forward by some in the party that a free enterprise system would somehow be intrinsically unfair to Black people. But he couldn't agree directly with Ferrar, so he contented himself by saying, 'America's a great country; it's achieved so much. It's truly amazing.' He smiled, and Ferrar grinned complicitly.

Ferrar began his campaigning in a quiet sort of way, walking out on the streets at nights, as if he was afraid of the sun affecting his complexion. He nodded in the dark to the few who greeted to him. Ben-Jamel shook his head pityingly and advised him, jokingly, as the elections drew closer, to take a flashlight: let people see how he looked. But, much to Ben-Jamel's surprise, this low-key approach paid off. People rushed up to Ferrar to congratulate him on running for office; he was genuinely surprised at the good feelings expressed. But one or two did mutter that he was a strange one, 'the leopard with many spots'. The story went round that he didn't want to show his spots in daylight, that he was afraid of the sunshine, thinking his maggoty-whiteness would disappear in the sun, that only in the dark was his precious asset intact.

Ben-Jamel heard these rumours, smirked and, patting Ferrar on the shoulder, told him that campaigning had its ups and downs.

One of the ups was the effect Ferrar had on some women. They were curious about him, wanted to touch his skin. There seemed something light and playful about him in contrast to the lumpen heaviness of their husbands. What was more remarkable was that he seemed unthreatening to the husbands. When he teased them, 'See, your wives, they're in love with me', sweetness was in the air, camaraderie.

Ben-Jamel, recalling his own vigorous youth, said a little wistfully, 'They're giving themselves fully to you, Ferrar. Like a sacrifice.'

But for Ferrar, play was play. Politics was about roads, sewers, bridges, irrigation systems, housing, education. No one had ever talked to the people about these things in such a candid manner before. When he said that he'd take the concerns of the district to the national parliament, no one doubted his sincerity.

On Ben-Jamel's advice, Ferrar held a large public meeting in the market square. He spoke passionately of the need for healing between the races, for honesty in government, and competence and service in administration. His audience drank in his words, but even as they listened to him, they kept looking at his face, hands and arms, where his shirt sleeves were rolled up. They commented on the spots on his face which seemed to grow larger the more he stayed out in the sunshine. He was one of their own, though neither European, African or Indian! They warmed to his self-deprecating humour when, responding to the heckling, he called himself a spotted cow — not a leopard or jaguar — and said that they should understand he meant both bovine sexes by this word, and that he was proud of the comparison, since the cow symbolised heaven for the Hindus and was a veritable work horse in Africa!

Ben-Jamel smiled, secretly wishing the Leader of the Party were here to see Ferrar's performance and his transformation.

Now a new mood of tolerance prevailed. One could hear a Hindu businessman at his shop's entrance hailing his Afro-Guyanese Christian brother:

'This Ferrar is a godsend!'

'Yes, an angel among us.'

'He's the best of the candidates.'

This was readily agreed, though the candidate now running against him was an Indian when before it was an African. Suddenly race and party lines were being crossed — all because of Ferrar.

'We should have had politicians like him long ago,' said the African.

'A man of principle for sure,' replied the Indian.

Ben-Jamel, when he came to the district again, said to Ferrar, 'Everyone in the city has heard of your activities. The Leader is...'

'Pleased, no?'

'You must take things a little more easily. Don't overwork yourself.'

'The heat doesn't bother me,' said Ferrar reassuringly.

'One can get carried away, you know... the people, their sentiments, feelings.'

Ferrar smiled, said he knew what Ben-Jamel meant.

Ben-Jamel added that it was a pity the Chief Electoral Officer had decided to set the election day for the hottest month of the year.

'Not too many people campaign when it's so hot. It's like in Europe or Canada, setting the date for an election in the heart of winter,' he said reflectively. Ferrar suspected that he had been reading the *Times* again. Ben-Jamel tapped him on the shoulder: 'You've nothing to worry about. The people are on your side; the women, you see, will influence their husbands.'

But the truth was that the heat was starting to get to Ferrar, and he took to carrying a towel with him, which he wiped his face with from time to time. But though he drank copious quantities of lemonade, fanned himself with the towel and dabbed perspiration from his neck and face, there was no escaping the fact that his skin was becoming increasingly red.

Now a heckler called out, 'Are you a Portuguese, Mr Ferrar?'

A Portuguese? Very quickly, more questions came: Was he a Syrian, Chinese, European?

Ben-Jamel and Ferrar now discussed the major speech which Ferrar had to give on the eve of the elections: this would be the last chance to sway all the undecided voters. A huge crowd, all the press, would be there.

Ben-Jamel noted with some satisfaction that Ferrar actually seemed a little nervous now, because people from the city were coming to listen to him, and some journalists from as far away as the UK and America. Ferrar's speech might even be carried on internationally networked TV like CNN: his face shown around the world, the man from nowhere, a new kind of politician who was transforming these elections.

Ferrar said this would be the chance for him to put into practice all he'd learnt about public speaking — the right pauses, the appropriate quotes to make, the moments to be humorous (he had a stack of jokes crammed in his head); the

best way to play to the crowd: he'd become a real 'communica-
tor', he confided to Ben-Jamel.

Then Ben-Jamel said that unfortunately he couldn't be
present for this major speech. 'You see, Ferrar, the Comrade
Leader wants me in the capital right away!'

'He does?'

'You're a quick learner, Ferrar,' Ben-Jamel said, and tapped
the other confidentially on the shoulder and sped off.

When Ferrar walked onto the platform, he looked redder
than ever. As the cameras flashed in his eyes, he felt as if he
were a circus act which no longer matched its billing. In all his
life he'd never seen so many people together in the market
square. Suddenly he wanted Ben-Jamel beside him, feeling
more than a twinge of nervousness. Maybe he'd made a mistake
getting into politics; it was all a farce.

But the towel which he'd taken to carrying had become a new
source of support. The women had started bringing towels with
them and waving them to him as his symbol: the towel which
would wipe away the sweat from their lives. Here was a new age
dawning!

Encouraged, pushed forward by the sheer momentum of the
women's voices, Ferrar allowed himself to be gripped by his
vision. He felt a new courage and confidence. He was a real
pioneer: there in front of him were people of all races, all
shades, though mostly black and brown, people who for years
had felt so much animosity, acrimony, bitterness in their hearts
for people of the other group and here he was, the one who was
changing all that — a miracle-worker!

He exulted in his political mastery; the thought of giving it all
up was now far from his mind. The heat sweltered; the microphone swayed in front of him. Sweat poured down his face; he
looked around for a towel, groping, grabbing the one handed to
him. His voice, at first clear, became hoarse; see-sawing; a

heaviness in his throat.

He thought fleetingly of Ben-Jamel. Was he indeed meeting with the Leader this very moment? Who cared? He started laughing at his own jokes (he'd practised them well in advance) and, naturally, laughter came from the crowd, small sections first, then everyone else.

'Tell us about Communism?' someone yelled.

'Yes — 'bout that!'

He talked passionately about peace in the universe, and how transcendent love must prevail above political ideology. He hardly knew what he was saying or what was happening when a woman broke out in chanting prayer... 'Amen! Amen!' Ferrar kept drawing from some inner reserve the stuff of his listeners' dreams. Towels were raised high in the air.

'Harmony and love!' voices called out.

Then Ferrar, remembering the occasion, said quietly, 'You will be voting soon; neither for an African or an Indian, but you will be voting...'

'For a zebra,' a heckler cried. He must be from the opposition. The word hung in the air, a crystallisation of all he was or wasn't.

He laughed, and the audience laughed too. Now everything had come down to this moment. The women's voices rallied to his side, his name resounding: 'Fer-rar! Fer-rar! Far...Far!'

'A zebra without stripes or spots, maybe I am!' Ferrar managed.

A strong wind blew, making the microphone vibrate and hum. The cameras rolled, floodlights glaring. Ferrar smiled, waving his towel like a standard: 'My stripes are with you... all of you,' he cried.

He kept on saying this, despite the heckling, the laughter; he swabbed more sweat from his face and neck. He glimpsed reporters busily scribbling, remembered how once he had wanted to become a reporter... Now he felt both inside and outside himself, a reporter noting his own speech.

His voice was now a sheer husk, rasping. Suddenly, this was another speech, in Parliament, and Ben-Jamel and the Prime Minister himself were listening to him, though dead-pan, not signalling any response.

He cried out shrilly, coming back to the crowd in front of him, 'Look among yourselves; yes, look — you will see all my stripes. Yes, look, my friends!' He laughed in an almost desperate way. They must start examining their own feelings about race; if they could achieve racial harmony, everything would improve: improved yields of sugarcane, rice, vegetables.

'There'll never be better yields. No way!' cried a distraught heckler.

Ferrar knew that he was at his point of greatest test. He began telling them that he was the one they'd been waiting for all these years (though he didn't use the word 'messiah'). But as he wiped the sweat from his face, arms and neck, he suddenly realised he was no longer himself; his skin itched.

Then, as if not knowing what else to say, he added: 'I should've been in the House of Commons in London... but I am here with you instead, giving you my best, an albino in flesh and blood! I could have been in Washington instead, but I am here!'

Someone coughed hard: was it the Leader? Was he actually here? Was that a sign that he'd gone too far? Ferrar wasn't sure where he was for a moment as the lights dazzled his eyes, blurring the faces before him, but he heard distinctly enough when someone said:

'So he thinks he should be in London or Washington!'

Another said, 'He's an impostor; look at him good!'

The word 'impostor' hung in the air.

III

None of this affected the outcome of the election. Ferrar won a resounding victory. No one in the entire country had won by such a large majority.

Ben-Jamel came to him, after a two-week absence, and said: 'Ferrar, I thought you were trying to make a fool of us.'

'Whatever gave you such an idea?'

'Your speech... But you know, it was my idea that the Leader himself should hear you.'

Ferrar smiled.

'We trusted you, totally... I did.'

Ben-Jamel didn't tell Ferrar that the Leader had warned all in the inner cabinet that Ferrar would have to be discredited. The margin of victory was too astonishingly wide.

The rumours grew more insistent: Ferrar was an impostor. What Ben-Jamel did tell Ferrar was that he had to be prepared to cope with what the Opposition, now larger than before, would throw at him. He'd be the continual butt of the Opposition jokes: mixed stripes: zebra, brindled cow, etc.

Ferrar muttered, 'But I've won a landslide — may I remind you.'

Ben-Jamel smiled.

Ferrar added quickly, 'We must carry on with the task of rebuilding the country. It's long overdue.'

'The Leader, you see, may not go along with your ideas. Surely, you have thought about that...? Party discipline too, see.'

Ferrar dithered.

'But... '

'But what?'

'You will be supporting my ideas in the party...'

'That won't be so easy. You see, Ferrar, I'll be leaving for the USA soon. My children, daughters, have sponsored me... I have a son in New York, he wants me to live with him there. It's become, well, too volatile here.'

Ferrar seemed struck.

Ben-Jamel continued, 'I asked the Leader for a diplomatic posting, but he hasn't responded.' He smiled, trying to hide his embarrassment.

'You will be deserting us, Mr Ben-Jamel, after your long years in politics, your work in building this party.' Ferrar was now genuinely concerned.

Ben-Jamel was flattered. It was the first time someone had acknowledged this.

Ferrar added, 'I've come to rely on your advice, like an older brother. I'll be lost without you.'

Again Ben-Jamel allowed a smile to flit across his face.

'You will have the Leader, Ferrar; you must build a close relationship with him.'

'As you have done?'

Ben-Jamel nodded.

'But he sees me as an impostor.'

The two men stared at each other in the silence that followed. Ben-Jamel knew at that point that though he hadn't really made any definite arrangements for leaving the country (it was only a vague thought, stemming from the last telephone conversation he had with his daughter) he had to prevail on her to sponsor him. He imagined going to news stands each day and buying copies of all the various newspapers, and reading to his heart's content. No doubt he'd long for a word or story about his native land; he'd have to learn to live with that.

A month later, just before Ben-Jamel was about to leave the country — on the pretext of going on a holiday — Ferrar came to see him.

'I wanted to talk to you about this business of my being an impostor.'

'But you're not.'

'The Opposition is saying it more and more.'

'Never mind the Opposition; it's their job to criticise.'

'It's getting to me, Ben-Jamel. I've almost come to believe that it's true.'

'Don't allow it to.'

'But... you're leaving.'

'It's just a holiday; I deserve one.'

'You wanted a diplomatic posting; you yourself said that.'

Ben-Jamel once more smiled.

'I am quitting politics,' said Ferrar gravely.

'What in heaven's name for? You're a success.'

'I have had enough.'

Ben-Jamel glared at him. 'How can you say that. You've only just begun. I told you that politics had its ups and downs. I really expected you to have more courage!'

'I have other interests?'

'What other interests?'

'I am not sure... But I've been thinking about the media business...'

'The media? It's a politician that you are, Ferrar!'

'But you didn't listen to my best speech.'

But Ben-Jamel wasn't thinking about that; he merely muttered, 'That's where you will make your money; we all have!'

Ferrar shook his head; he was principled, was above corruption. He wanted to throw this at Ben-Jamel, a man, it seemed, he had mistakenly admired.

'You've won the largest majority in the history of this region, the entire Caribbean! You're the star on the horizon; you could be the saviour of our people! You could bring a new order; create a real transformation!'

Ben-Jamel wasn't sure why he was saying this, why he was so keen to persuade Ferrar to stay in politics, but he kept on at it, volubly.

'You — with the attraction the people have towards you, you will make it, Ferrar!'

Ferrar realised he wasn't getting anywhere with Ben-Jamel. But he was determined, he'd thought long and hard about quitting.

Then Ben-Jamel smiled. 'Ah, I know. You want to leave the country.'

Ferrar didn't answer.

'You do, man. Out with it!'

'The thought has crossed my mind.'

Ben-Jamel was secretly glad. It lessened his own feelings of guilt, and then he suddenly imagined Ferrar with him in Washington, and the two of them having tea every so often, and discussing affairs of the world. He would listen to Ferrar's opinions with encouraging interest, as, respectfully, Ferrar would listen to his. Maybe from time to time they'd reminisce about the past, over a glass of Demerara rum, about their lives here, in this place, this country.

Then Ferrar said that for the time being he'd remain to help the Indian man, Kumar, run for office in the coming by-election.

'Not Blair, the African?'

'Him too.'

'Both at the same time?'

'Oh, I have already talked to them... they will have to take turns. It's the only way.' He smiled.

Ben-Jamel didn't. He figured they were back where they'd started.

Ferrar wiped more perspiration from his face.

'And after that, where will you go?'

'Back to the interior, where I came from... remember?'

Ben-Jamel nodded; he'd forgotten. But he couldn't see Ferrar in the interior. He was with the lawyers and judges, drinking good whisky and talking politics.

When Ben-Jamel reported this conversation to the Leader, just before he left, they'd laughed almost as uncontrollably as the Prime Minister and the Leader of the Opposition had laughed when the former had passed on this report at one of their secret meetings. It had, of course, been at the Prime Minister's suggestion that the opposition had attacked Ferrar so mercilessly.

'...and let us hope Mr Ferrar has the leisure, holed up in the interior, to consider his foolishness', the Leader had written in a note to Ben-Jamel, which the latter was reading in the plane crossing the Atlantic. In the plane, Ben-Jamel felt as if he was nowhere, and he suspected that America would feel like this too. But he knew he'd never return, though he'd no doubt think about his creation, Ferrar, from time to time: his alter ego?

ANTICS OF THE INSANE

Where the idea that living in the tropics causes madness came
from, I didn't know. Was it that the intense heat and humidity
was supposed to addle the brain? Maybe. With Uncle, you
might have wondered whether madness was contagious. He
started showing 'signs' not long after he started working at the
'Mad House' — more 'properly' the psychiatric hospital close
to our main town. It was the only one of its kind in the entire
country. People made fun of it, as they made fun of the 'mad
people'. Some said it was the only legacy the British left us after
they departed, finished with the tropics. Now, we would take
over!

At the 'Mad House,' Uncle's job was to look after the
unfortunates, though I suspect he too laughed at or, at best,
humoured them. It was mostly Afro-Guyanese who worked
there, being near the town, and folk-wisdom had it that only they
were capable of taking care of the mentally ill — Uncle being
the one exception. It was a distinction which gave him some
status in our village. Auntie watched Uncle proudly as he talked
about the insane to our neighbours. When he rode off to work
in his uniform, he was a far cry from the regular sugarcane
workers and rice-farmers around. It all added to the air of
intrigue which surrounded him. When the neighbours laughed,

Auntie laughed loudest; and when Uncle wasn't there, she told them how he pretended to be insane himself: the leer of his mouth, jaw dropping, lips hanging: the signs of unmistakable madness or retardation. She was offended, though, when a neighbour suggested that working too long in the 'Mad House' could cause him to become 'tainted'. She was even heard to say, 'Look at them — they not mad!' — meaning the Afro-Guyanese who worked there, a much more generous estimate of their mental capacities than she was accustomed to make.

So, for a while, she was content when Uncle came home in the afternoons to regale her with more stories about the 'mad people'. It was as if he worked there only to pick up stories and bring them home to her.

Then the stories began to be about Uncle himself. Auntie no longer laughed. Now she started looking out for 'signs' in him: each quirk of behaviour, gesture that was out of the ordinary. But Auntie also knew that people were malicious, especially Indians. Things, though, really seemed to change when Uncle became involved in the hospital cricket team, which, at first, I thought, was really for the good.

Uncle, wiry, thin and agile behind the wicket, was quickly given the nickname the 'Dancing Master' by those who watched him and admired the way he moved: legs and hands and hips, suddenly springing up like an alert cat on the fast-moving ball! At home, Uncle would simulate being behind the wicket as I watched and applauded.

Auntie smiled.

Now it was if Uncle had been born with that nickname; and even Auntie, in jest, sometimes called him 'Dancing Master'.

I often wished I could go and watch him play; but the Mad House was too far away to walk to, and I could only listen to the stories being told about him, his moving left and right as the fast bowler pounced down the wicket and beat the batsman. Sometimes I pretended to be Uncle, moving real fast, calling myself the Dancing Master and imagining the Barbadian legend Wesley Hall doing the fast bowling.

Auntie watched me and frowned.

Now Uncle had got into the habit of bringing home his friends for a spree after each cricket match, a celebration which sometimes lasted five or six hours. Auntie dreaded this, because Uncle usually provided the drinks and food, mainly curried chicken. When, after each pay-day, cricket match or not, a spree followed, Uncle's wallet quickly became empty. Auntie, melodramatic, lachrymose, wrung her hands.

Uncle only shrugged.

'You, man!' Auntie bawled. 'You jus' like dem mad people in the hospital!'

The Dancing Master shook his head and laughed, pulling a face.

Auntie yelled, 'Yes — you jus' like them!'

The neighbours expressed their concern. There were real 'signs' now. Uncle seemed thinner, wasted. People said he should stop working at the hospital. But Uncle, sober the next morning, laughed hard, and next pay-day brought home his cronies again, all town people, black people, the villagers noted disapprovingly, bent on enjoying themselves.

Auntie watched each one with a surly expression, suspicion written across her face. But the cronies didn't mind, they simply wanted to have a good time. Uncle made sure of that, lavishing more food and drink and, by his own looks, encouraging Auntie to keep her silence. When he was almost drunk, I noted, he had a strange command over her.

'They're all good-for-nothing!' Auntie fired when everyone had gone.

The next morning, Uncle rolled over in the bed as Auntie repeated all she had said the previous night.

'Those men you bring here — is all a part of you' madness!'
Uncle merely rubbed his eyes.

'You mad, jus' like them.'

Uncle yawned.

Then one evening, as if he could suddenly stand it no longer, he said: 'Maybe I am mad.'

'Show me you' madness then!' Auntie yelled, as if suddenly unsure whether Uncle was simply masking wilful disobedience with show, or whether he was genuinely mad.

Uncle laughed.

'Yes, show me, man!'

'Wait, you go see!'

Then the drinking parties ended and I knew that his cricketing days were over, and that I'd no longer see him play in a test match, no longer watch him show off all he was capable of to large crowds at Lords, Brisbane, Delhi or Lahore. I wouldn't hear his name on the radio, the BBC, as I had longed, one day, to hear. Now, for sure, he wouldn't be playing alongside Kanhai, Sobers or Walcott. Uncle had become quiet, withdrawn even, a shadow of his dancing-master days. I was really starting to become disappointed in him.

Auntie, though, was glad to see him sober — and sane; I knew she dreaded waking up one morning and finding him really mad! Then Uncle started talking again about the antics of the insane, a grain of rice lodged between his front teeth after he finished eating.

'You got to see them to believe,' he said. I was staying with them regularly now: they didn't have any children of their own.

'Who?' I asked, harshly.

'The mad people.'

I looked at him, without smiling.

He made a face, as if trying to scare me: 'Those people; it's how they look!'

I didn't flinch.
He laughed.

Outside in the yard Auntie cried, 'Chick-chick-chick!' She had taken to raising chickens, and they had become, in addition to Uncle, her constant anxiety. They were always threatening to take sick and die. She had begun saying that Uncle should take some responsibility for them.

I watched Auntie's and Uncle's behaviour closely. I liked them both; they were different. I'd heard from mother, for instance, that their marriage hadn't been arranged (as hers was), and that Uncle had courted Auntie by climbing up a jamun tree, and each time Auntie passed underneath he had howled at her like a monkey — so my mother said. I laughed loudly at this, and from time to time I imagined Uncle up the tree.

Now she was outside, shrieking: 'Chick-chick-chick!' and looking for signs of disease, whilst Uncle had retired to his bed to read.

Then Auntie went back upstairs to peek at Uncle who, I knew, would be reading a Jehovah's Witness text. He liked the pictures of the birds, tame lions, deer standing alongside a fig-leaved Adam and Eve who were patting the animals' heads in benign tranquillity. Those birds were very different from the scrawny ones outside.

'It will come — the Day of Judgement,' Uncle muttered another time, when he was reading, knowing Auntie was close by.

Auntie grimaced. She took him seriously and Uncle took advantage of that.

'You mad, man!' she fired back.

'It will come, when the Lord will separate the sheep from the goats.'

'Eh?'

Uncle grinned.

'Shut up, man!'

'Yes, who're the sheep and who're the goats?' He looked at me and winked.

'You're one of the goats. You, man!' Auntie snapped. Then she ran down the stairs and started feeding the chickens again.

'CHICK-CHICK-CHICK!'

Uncle went to the window and looked out. The chickens were clustered around Auntie's legs, like obedient children. 'Chick-chick-chick!' Auntie continued in a half-shriek to the ones that didn't eat, their heads bent low to the ground.

'He should look after the chickens, that man!' cried Auntie, fretting louder when I went outside to join her.

Then sickness really did strike the chickens. Auntie fretted incessantly, but Uncle merely shrugged, muttered something to himself, and took off for the Mad House on his Raleigh bicycle (one of the ladies' kind without the bar in the middle).

Auntie watched him going off, then looked at the chickens and moaned. 'They'll die! They'll all die!' A strange growth was forming on the chickens' beaks and this hampered their appetite.

I watched Auntie, how sad she looked. 'They will all die,' she moaned.

When Uncle came home that afternoon, he at once said: 'They won't die!'

'They will!' said Auntie. 'There's too much sin in this house!'

I wasn't sure what Auntie meant by that. Maybe she remembered Uncle's talk about the Day of Judgement.

Uncle slowly started going up the stairs, looking crumpled. We'd realised he'd taken to drinking again, though he did none of it at home.

Later that afternoon I watched Uncle examining each chicken, pulling at the beaks, muttering to himself about which ones would die and which wouldn't. Some of the chickens were slumped in a corner, unable to walk; others remained in the coop, hardly coming out, no matter how much I tried to coax them. One opened its eyes widely, as if that was all.

Auntie lamented: 'That man, he wouldn't do anything. But he can play doctor for mad people.'

I imagined Uncle slowly turning the pages of his Jehovah's Witness text in his room.

Auntie coughed hard. 'Why he doesn't do something about these chickens, only God knows!'

The more she talked, the more melodramatic she became: one would think for Auntie the chickens were humans. Now I watched her beat her breast and lament as she lifted up one, two, then three dead chickens — still hoping they'd live.

Uncle came home from work earlier than usual the next day, looking serious. He carried a handbag with him. I watched him hop off the Raleigh bicycle and walk into the yard.

Auntie wasn't around, she was somewhere in the kitchen; she hadn't seen him come.

I quickly went over to him, suspecting he was up to something. I smelled rum on his breath.

He looked at me and he knew I knew.

He grinned.

'You home early,' I said.

'Shh!'

I became more curious.

'Where is she?'

I pointed upstairs to the kitchen.

Then he walked deliberately to the hens' coop, went inside, and opened the handbag. He took out an injection needle and tested the point with his finger.

I held my breath.

Somehow I'd already figured what he'd do. He'd talked about injecting his patients from time to time as part of his duties, and I'd yearned to see him at it.

'Ha, now you will see a real doctor at work.'

I sensed he'd drunk less than usual, but his hands shook nevertheless.

He crouched forward, going closer to the helpless-looking chickens.

Uncle grinned. 'Look good, boy, at a real doctor!'

I leaned closer behind him. Something told me I ought to run upstairs and bawl out for Auntie to come see! Instead, I remained watching him.

Uncle deliberately parted the feathers of one chicken, then pressed the needle into the bird's thigh. The chicken's eyes widened, canted in a sudden swivelling motion, then closed heavily.

'Ha,' he grinned, 'it's easier than I thought.'

Another chicken.

He was becoming more confident now.

There were fifteen chickens in the coop, and Uncle injected each one, moaning with satisfaction each time he pressed the long needle into their flesh.

'Now we will see!' he let out.

I sighed hard.

Uncle, gloatingly, walked up to his room.

Auntie appeared at the door; she was suspicious at once. I wanted to tell her right away about Uncle's deed, but remained tight-lipped.

'That man,' she muttered, 'I hope he sleeps well. But why he doesn't take care of the chickens? He just doesn't care.' She was speaking to no one in particular.

I looked at her, and thought about Uncle injecting each

chicken, and the chicken's eyes swivelling. I wondered about the patients under his care, imagined him pressing the needle into each arm... then once more thought how he carefully pulled the feathers aside and injected the chicken's flesh.

That night I dreamt the chickens were running around excitedly in the yard: they were everywhere, even coming into the house, up and down, fluttering and flapping their wings: each one healthily alive. And Auntie, gleeful; I'd never seen her so happy before. Her hands full of rice, she scattered it wide and called out loudly, 'Chick-chick-chick!'

I woke up early the next morning; Auntie wasn't up yet. I knew Uncle was still in bed; he was always the last to wake.

Then I heard Auntie stir.

'Where are you?' she called out to me.

'Downstairs.'

'How are the chickens?'

I walked towards the coop.

'Will tell you when I see them,' I shouted back.

'Hurry up — I want to know!'

Inside the coop, I noticed that the chickens, all the ones Uncle had injected, were lying still as stone. They were a far cry from the sprightly chickens in my dream.

I counted fifteen dead chickens.

Auntie: 'Why don't you answer, boy?'

I stood looking at the dead chickens for a while.

Auntie was coming down the stairs now. She had a handful of rice; she still let herself hope that the chickens had weathered their sickness and would be ready to run about healthily again.

I walked out of the coop and faced Auntie.

'Well?' she demanded.

I didn't answer.

'What about the chickens, boy?'

'They are...'

'They are what?' But in Auntie's question, and the way her expression changed, I figured she knew at once.

I wondered then if I should tell her about Uncle's injections.

She began marching up the stairs, hands akimbo, mouth twisted into a grimace that was really frightening.

I knew then that she knew!

I heard Uncle's voice — strange that he was up so early — 'How are the chickens?' A wide grin swept across his face, a lingering gloat.

Maybe he was thinking of telling his cronies at the Mad House about his work with the chickens, and their laughing loudly and congratulating him. Now, oddly, he seemed to be in command, or at least out of the reach of Auntie's rage.

She, indeed, appeared confused as she looked at him. Then she turned and looked at me, and looked back at Uncle.

Uncle continued to grin. 'The Day of Judgement has come...' He laughed loudly, his eyes bright.

I looked at Auntie, waiting for her to bawl out at him, her screech at fever pitch. But her lips merely kept twisting, her cheeks looking as if they were about to be sucked in in a strange paroxysm; and no words came out.

Then slowly she started walking back downstairs to the coop. The word 'sign' was on her lips.

Next she lifted each dead chicken high in her hand, still with that same expression on her face, and repeated the word 'sign' — as if for all the neighbours to see and hear.

Uncle merely kept gloating, like the victor of some contest, as he surveyed the ground where the chickens had once scampered about.

RITUAL OF FIRE

They pulled the heavy-tailed reptile out of the murky brown water and spread it out on the bank not far from us. I took in the creature's ribbed skin, slowly swishing board-stiff tail, jaws opening, teeth like short sharp spears. A tremor went through me, and I had to look away. The jaws widened, then suddenly snapped shut with a heavy thud.

So many times before I'd imagined reptiles, large and small, crawling in and out of the creek's murky depths; sometimes even coming into our house. I'd bite my lips, grind my teeth with fear. 'Look, look!' the other children would cry, pointing to the water. 'Look... there! See, the eyes lookin' back!' The reptiles kept crawling into my dreams.

Now this one: the real thing, eyes like billiard balls, jaws slowly opening again, holding me to it even in the sun's overpowering heat. I started sweating as the creature turned, as if still twisting amid the water and weeds.

The other children were jeering, revelling in the capture. Now they'd make absolutely sure it was dead. What inner fear did they mask with their laughter?

Now adults were coming out, a real crowd gathering round the beast. I watched it, fearing it would suddenly lunge at me. Water all around, rising up, and I was submerging, overwhelmed. I couldn't call out, though I could hear the sound of my words fully formed in my head.

More jeers, laughter. 'Fire,' I heard. 'Yes, let's get a fire goin'!' Different signals rushed to my brain, just as overwhelming, but I was no longer submerging or drowning.

'Now we'll see if it's really alive,' another cried.

Eyes were lit up in many of the faces. All about me was the creek's blackness-browness; the tangle of water hyacinths and other tufted weeds springing out with long hairs. I was pulling at the thick strands, trying to get free.

'Yes, a fire!' I heard twenty or thirty voices at once, but distant from me, as if my blood was beating with half a heart, as if I was breathing with only one lung. Suddenly I didn't want the creature to die. I looked around in dismay. I saw the fire; the flames rising; my own words etched in my head.

Then I saw the man who had shot the beast, a solitary, aloof man. He had taken a long, calculated, determined aim. The gun had exploded suddenly: the entire creek jolted, the reptile somersaulting, a whitish stomach protruding a few seconds later above the water.

He was watching me intently, a slight grin on his face. Did he know what I was thinking? Smoke, smouldering; the air sulphur, the creature writhing. I put my hands to my eyes, I didn't want to see any more.

But from the crowd the cries for fire increased, from young and old alike, though the women were shouting the loudest as they pulled at their hair and clothes.

'Oh, God,' I let out, mutely.

The man who had shot the beast stood alone, hands folded. He couldn't agree with what they wanted to do, could he? Or was he the one giving the orders to have the reptile roasted alive? He had spent so long looking for the beast, night and day. Was it because he hated it? I'd watched him hunting for it a number of times before; I'd imagined the reptile moving, slowly re-entering the creek, disappearing forever.

Someone nudged me. 'Look at the fire! You en' see it?' The flames faltered, started again, shot up in the air. Now sun and fire were one. I looked around at the youths whooping it up, waiting to see the alligator's tail twitch — the nerve-endings' reaction — and then singing out, 'It na dead yet!' I inhaled the acrid smell of gunpowder, my eyes falling on an empty cartridge, studying it in a daze.

The creature's tail suddenly twitched again. It was as if my own skin was burning; I cringed, convulsed.

'Look, see, how it twist an' turn,' another called.

The sun glittered through green leaves from an overhanging cochineal tree; the creek wound narrowing to a neck; rotten sugar cane smells, sickly sweet, mixed with the smell of burning flesh.

My stomach heaved as I saw the flames eating into the reptile's hard, corrugated skin; etching the scalloped flesh. I saw the eyelids quivering, the creature's and mine: the fire taking over my day-dreams.

NO!

I kept shouting, though my tongue was heavy-laden.

Someone pushed me forward, someone from the outer circle, and I was in the centre of this merry-go-round, the flames still rising, smouldering, hotter than ever. The alligator splashed in my head, its leviathan might hurling water high against the bank, reaching as far as the stilts of the houses.

I stared, waiting for the tail to twitch again.

'See, it almost dead now.'

Impulsively, I drew closer, now part of the crowd's swirling presence. I looked at the creature's face, the ribbed, knobby eyelids — the sheer ugliness of it, yet with an arresting beauty all its own; the groove of skin, serrations along the sides of the head; a darkish neck tapering to a white underside.

The fire was still ablaze, close to its tail, like an unnatural appendage. The searing pain of the bullets driving through the neck, the stomach; splattering flesh: corpuscles and sinews pitched everywhere in water and mud: I felt it all.

The cry went up louder.

I kicked at the dust, wishing for rain, as if all my life depended on it. All my attention was on this creature on the shallow ground, earth reclaiming it. The tail still twitched in spasms, moments of living energy. Then, silence.

I stiffened with pain. Water, water... the flame had to be put out. I sensed eyes watching me. Hands reaching out to me.

Suddenly, a loud boom... the gun firing. My heartbeat quickened. Viscera and bone-marrow throbbed; I was shot, torn limb by limb.

'It not dead yet!' came a cry.

'No... it not!'

'Look — it na move; it dead-dead now!'

Voices resounded like the trumpet call of a thousand birds invisible in the embroidered net and eye of the forest. I opened my eyes, looking at the dead beast's head. I saw my own stupefaction and bewilderment in its eyes, the knobby eyelids rolled back, as if in disdain of death.

I stamped my feet heavily on the hard ground; cuffed at my sides, arms flailing, tears streaming down my face, in a tantrum all my own. Then I realized I was the focus of the attention; not the reptile.

I looked around for the hunter.

Where was he? The sun had now slunk away like a conspirator, after the foul deed was done. I dug a hole in the ground with my toes, inch by inch, fists clenched. Eyes were still on me: the alligator's dead, rolled-back eyes piercing into me.

Then I sensed him coming towards me, his hand touching me, reassuring me in a whisper. I wanted the beast to start crawling back into the water; to splash about, create waves mightier than anyone had ever seen; whirlpools amidst the blaze.

I muttered silently as he held my hand, whispering, 'It will be all right.' He, the killer of the beast!

I looked at him.

'Well, sorta. It'll be there again, in the water, swimming. Watch out for it!' He drawled his words, grinning, as if he had known all along this would happen.

I tried to pull away. But he held me firmly. 'No, you mustn't go. You must—'

'Mus' what?'

'Listen.'

'Listen?'

I kept pulling away.

'Wait,' he growled, face set hard.

I looked at the gun slung across his shoulder, like a living thing with a mouth, a body. He smiled, inviting me to touch the barrel, to rub my palm against it.

I did — quickly.

'You see,' he said, 'it not really dead. It can be everywhere at de same time.'

'Yes, it's alive!' I said quickly.

But it was as if he was talking to himself, his voice strained. 'It'll drift into the weeds, grass, leaves, for miles.'

I continued to run my fingers against the gun's barrel, imagining the loud blast, which wasn't like a blast any more. More like a soft cry.

Again, he knew what I was thinking; he let go of my arm. He knew I wanted to be free.

I started walking away: something propelling me. I walked faster, a million eyes on my back: eyes of people, reptiles; all coming behind, at my command.

I walked on, sweat dripping down my back. But I was also shivering. In the silence, the trees rustled. I heard his voice again, in a kind of parody and dead-seriousness.

'Everything go be okay, eh. Yes, wait na — you will see;

everything go be okay after a time.'

I wanted to tell him that what he was saying wasn't true. Yet I kept on walking, hurrying, the wind blowing across the Atlantic: mudcrabs, molluscs, shrimp in the air: the distinctive tang of seawater, crabgrass.

I started feeling a sense of relief, though a million things were still following me: I was carrying the entire elemental world, a Pied Piper.

Then I was entering a narrow cave, some place where I'd be confined, but it didn't matter because all the reptiles were with me; I'd nurture, protect them, as much as they'd protect me.

BOOM!

The gun fired again. He was still laughing. Crucifier! I was pulling my arm away from him.

People were gathered around me. 'You passed out. You had a sunstroke.' A man bent down, concerned.

'No,' I denied. 'I didn't pass out. I can remember everything.' I felt as if only the world had been asleep. 'The alligata... it really dead?'

'Yes,' came the quick answer from someone standing close by.

'Is it really?' I felt it was still alive, its large eyes, like solid moons, looking back at me from under knobby eyelids.

Laughter again from the people around me.

'What about him?'

'Who?' They looked at me, puzzled.

'The one with the gun?'

They knew who I was talking about. They were still laughing.

'He's not here. He gaan.'

But I remembered his hands gripping my wrist, his words to me.

'Why he leave?'

'Maybe he afraid of you,' someone said to a chorus of mocking laughter.

'No,' I hissed. I looked into the canal, the weeds; sensed an underwater turbulence, the creatures below, turning, turning. When I could bear it no longer, I looked away.

'You... you turn strange again, no?' one said.

'I am not!'

They started walking away, laughing, but leaving me alone.

I kept thinking of the hunter, the boom of the gun in my ears. I looked into the creek once more, saw him looking at me, the gun still pointing. I saw the water starting to rise, a commotion underway: the boardstiff tail splashing hard. But I knew it would be a long time before this happened.

BERBICE CROSSING

A wet wind, then lightning, thunder. The heavier rains came and Auntie yelled, 'Get dem all before they're wet! Get dem all!'

We rushed helter-skelter to gather the clothes spread out on the barbed-wire fence surrounding the yard. We were in Grandmother's house, and Auntie screeched deafeningly as the rains came down more heavily, the wind slapping against our faces. Meanwhile, Grandmother was sitting on the makeshift balcony, despite the rain, nursing an invalid condition as she talked to herself in Hindi, though not to her own mother, an ancient and sinewy bundle in the cowdung-plastered bottom-house.

The rain thrashed about, slapping shingles, windows, jalousies; the galvanised zinc roof throbbed as Auntie yelled, mouth askew, gums pink, 'Get them all!' as pants, shirts, bed sheets – some torn – were pulled from the barbed wire. I made a face at her, and at all the world, as the rain pelted down harder. Not long after, I walked outside in the thick mud, the once hard ground slippery and treacherous. I rolled around, my hands, knees, feet plastered with mud; I inhaled the dank odour, its sogginess like glue.

Huddled in my room with a blanket over my head, I day-dreamed of the sugar cane fields not far from our house burning luridly, a salve against the rain's onslaught. Auntie at last was silent. Outside, the trade winds fluttered against the red jhandi flag, an emblem of ancestry and belief. Black ash from the burnt cane floated about like a million drunk tarantulas. I reached out to catch the brittle strands disintegrating against the windows, jalousies and floors. An acrid smell rose in the air. As for Grandmother, she remained quietly fretting in the rising humidity, still echoing: 'Get dem all before it's too late.'

I pulled the blanket over my head, thinking of escape.

I am running along a foreign street, free from mud and pools of rainwater, feeling the firm, asphalted, hard ground under the heavy boots I wear to protect me from the ice and snow.

Auntie came and stood at the door of my room, hands akimbo, tightening her lips, murmuring, 'See, you'll come to no good!' My quickfire, 'I'll never return!' was hurled only at her departing back.

I am on a small raft, alone on the Berbice, the river's waves leaping high, the raft bobbing up and down, sometimes submerging. My eyes closed, I am being thrown about into unconsciousness. When I come to, I am in a deserted place, mudcrabs scuttling about by the dozen. I stay here: an outcast, eking out an existence by snaring fish and crabs; eating coconut jelly; seeking out wild fruits and nuts. I hide out of sight, only once in a while coming out into the open. Auntie (and my mother) wring their hands in despair. I only allow Grandmother to see me; she smiles in her secret way, she understands how I feel.

But I was soon to lose this closeness with Grandmother. My mother and I moved away to town and one of Grandmother's legs was amputated because of her diabetes. She retreated into her grimaces and gestures. I recall the pain in her bloodshot eyes.

My mother and I visited her, my mother with grimaces of her own — which also became mine.

Auntie, with the *beata* — a slab of wood — in her hand at the edge of the murky-brown canal not far from our house, raised it once more against the soiled clothes, shirt buttons flying in the air. A thick cluster of drifting water hyacinths, mucka-mucka, drew closer in the sun's brilliance.

'See,' said Auntie, 'what I been telling you. She bound to die one day.' She meant Grandmother. 'And what will you do then, eh? Tell me that!' The *beata* raised again, she pounded out a rhythm on the clothes against my wayward coming and going, crabs caught at the far end of the Berbice river dangling from my finger tips. She, who'd never travelled beyond the district, what did she know of foreign ways? Waves in my mind. Again the *beata*, raised. 'Maybe you will leave here one day. An' *we'll* get all de crabs,' she whined.

What, indeed, was I going to do? I pretended not to be anywhere at all, though I was dream-travelling now to America. Going, and yet not going. To Britain, Canada.

I am lost in foreign streets: an *alien*, the immigration officer eying me suspiciously. At Newfoundland Harbour, in Canada, I study an iceberg that bulges against the horizon, apparently permanently stuck there. An unwelcoming? Next I am part of prairie anonymity with endless fields of wheat.

'The crabs will never go wid you!' Auntie added.

'They will!' I called back.

The others around me, those who also wanted to leave, laughed hard, cheeks widening, stretched tight. Auntie's *beata* was raised again, the veins in her hands standing out. An alligator amid the cluster of mucka-mucka drew closer. The slab of wood, tightly held in her hand, came down hard. The jaws widened in the driftwood-like head of the reptile, prehistory itself. *Oh God, look out!* Auntie's wrist locked in those powerful jaws: blood pouring out. Auntie's hand in tatters, white bone exposed.

'You not one o' us!' she insisted, despite the pain.

A dream world far across the Berbice, the vast Atlantic. Auntie's voice retreating, just when I longed for her to be shrill. Snow falling in a whirl close to Lake Superior: Nanabijou, aboriginal old man of the mountains, lying still for centuries amid the shale and rocks. A reservation's Great Spirit at Mount McKay. Ice-breakers throbbing hard to free the wheat-laden ships on the lake; steel against the elemental ice-force. Auntie, do you hear? High buildings, downtown office towers; Duluth close-by, not far from New York, my imagination walking down Wall Street, Fifth Avenue. Toronto next, my climbing up the CN Tower. The self-exiled man from the Caribbean, lost in the Empire, who now berated me: 'You say you are *bilingual*, yet you only speak English — and *rubbish!*'

Dialectal laughter.

In Canada I continue to cultivate a creole tongue — like a parody — with further accents in the snow. And still the blanket's over my head, my tongue mute. Now by Toronto's Eaton Centre on a hot summer's day, I hear voices of the diaspora: someone declaiming against the government's inaction over his refugee status; then a hot-gospeller's *Sisteren an' brethren, you'll soon be bona fide Canadian citizens. It's time for another amnesty! You'll not be an illegal immigrant forever! GIVE! GIVE!* Next a Jamaican-Rastafarian in the Jane-Finch area, Downsview, *You hear the police siren?*

'This is a racist country, brother!' calls out another. But Auntie, in the audience, camouflaged in dark glasses, laughs.

Another heckler: 'They should send all-you refugees to live in igloos up north, and let's see how black men can date women with blubber!'

'I am a blasted Canadian citizen! No one's gonna tell me to move from Toronto!' cries another.

'Man, you're just a hyphenated Canadian. Ask Multiculturalist Canada. You'll never be a real Canadian!'

'But I... I used to plant trees, trap bears in British Columbia and Northwestern Ontario!'

'Not jaguars?'

(Heh-Heh-Heh)

Again, Grandmother, phantom-legged, on the balcony, watching the canefields burning, strands of ash floating like strange confetti. Auntie still chomping at the bit because of imminent rain, *beata* in hand, mightier whacks in the sun's distant eye.

Her thighs fleshy as she slept wide-eyed, dress hitched-up over her knees; my own shame for my youthful desire, the blanket pulled firmly over my head.

Down the full length of the Canje, a tributary of the Berbice: Magdalenenburg, where the first real slave rebellion in the Caribbean took place in 1763. Slaves crying out: Who will liberate us? Coffy and Akara? Here, at the edge of the town, at the umbilicus of my mother's house, life goes on in its desultory way, though once in a while awakened by an overseas telephone call from one of those sometimes similarly ramshackle houses with foreign voices whirring in them. New York, London, Toronto, do you hear?

'You there, Ma?'

'Is you, Son?'

'I am calling from New Yawk.'

'New... YAWK?'

(*Squawk-quack-quawk*)

A telephone pole leaning over, wires dangling close to the jhandi pole, red flag fluttering for Hanuman. Is it a symbol of

revolutionary communism the British troops wonder? Cheddi
Jagan, do you hear?

'You not calling from Toronto, Son?'

'I am here in New Yawk for a week.'

'Son, when last me see you? When you go come home? Me
gat pain, Son.'

'Get some more medicine.'

'Where?'

'At the drug store.'

'They all empty, got nothin' here.'

Mud, swamps, rice fields. Ethnic strife with Indians and
Africans asserting ownership over this place, the drums beating
out rhythms against my own skin. I see the tremor of my
mother's lips, the shake of her hands, her fear of lurking
violence.

'Me scared bad, Son. Me go dead an' me na go see you face
again.'

'I will come home soon.'

'You will?'

The airport's particular tension, place of escape; constant
blackout; streets jagged, potholed, without asphalt; all in the
sun's dappled eye; the land dried, crusted hard; vultures
circling in a dizzying spiral, seeking out a rank smell, carcass
of a faltered animal: raccoon or anteater, dog or sheep?

Now literally here, looking at my mother's seeming lack of
recognition. Who was I? As if I was still in New York, Toronto
with their wide streets, high-rises, factories; subway systems,
jam-packed commuters.

'Ma, is me!'

She stretches out a hand bunched with knotted blood vessels.

'Me glad you come back home, Son.'

'Where's Auntie?'

Beata, her hand raised; buttons still suddenly flying out like missiles. My memory's refrain.

Rain again, falling on a wayward rooftop. A blanket once more pulled over my head. Humming like bees of doubt, my mother's endless questions. What was Canada really like? America? They're the same, no? England, Europe? Unfamiliar place-names. My mother insisting, 'Tell me more, Son.' A collective cry in my ears which I'd carried with me to Canada and America, throughout the long winters, tundra everywhere, moss carpeting the fir-and- jackpine reforested ground.

Silence in this enclosed cauldron of tropical heat. Some other places: worlds. Welcome Paris, Bonn, Hamburg, Tokyo — but not Bombay, Harare, Lagos, Kingston.

'You t'ink I could ever live in America, Son?'

I'm thinking about the ancient old lady, once indentured, in the cowdung-splattered bottom-house, with pellagra blotched skin. Then an escalator moving: she at the bottom, petrified, not sure what to do. Her legs would be chewed in! Oh God! A Bramalea City Centre shopping mall crowd, not far from the Pearson International Airport, people looking away from her, too embarrassed to help. She mutely muttering prayers, mantras, invoking Ram, Krishna: the full pantheon of the *Ramayana* in this Christian-Jewish land.

Someone, please help her!

She's stepping into an elevator and being whizzed up at a frightening speed to the penthouse of the Empire State Building. Or was it Toronto's CN Tower?

Oh God, stop it please!

The temperate sun's shining moment. All the while Auntie was still at the water's edge, *beata* in hand. All movements of a sort. My mother waiting, breathing harder. Unwelcoming, welcoming; ah, she was glad I had returned. She wanted to know about Ottawa, Canada's capital. Was I really called a 'visible minority', 'South Asian'? Toronto, Vancouver, Montreal: was I

just a statistic, always advocating affirmative action? I was also
a *Black*, the government's computer print-out said.

'We did right to leave there,' a Ghanaian said to me, meaning
the tropics. Monty would take me to a strip-club in the nearby
town of Gatineau to watch heavyweight fights on the big screen;
he disliked Mike Tyson. Nude white women dancing: just a
passing interest. Next on stage, a dusky-skinned girl from
Montreal (Cuban father, French-Canadian mother), doing her
gyrations as the males hissed ecstatically. Monty shrugged and
calmly called her a 'sister'.

'All that ass!' a white male blurted out.

Monty seemed suddenly inspired...'Neo-African Canada',
his brain-wave. Yes, he'd invite people from all races, including a young Japanese girl — the 'flower' of the group — to help
him form such an organization to start a new Canada.

'All that ass!' hissed again.

My mother was listening to me in the hum of a faraway
silence. Monty's next scheme was to try to solve the Third
World's economic woes by setting up toy-exchange stores,
which he'd franchise; all the discarded Canadian children's
toys would be sent to the Third World at Christmas. 'It won't
work,' a Jamaican said to him. 'African women don't spoil their
kids the way white Canadian women do.'

'Monty, maybe you should sponsor your mother to come
here,' Iris, his white girlfriend, a psychology major, said.

'Immigration's too much of a hassle,' he replied calmly. He
admitted to me that he didn't like the idea of dragging the entire
Third World to Canada. Where would people go next? Even
further up north?

All that blubber!

Iris moaned, telling a story about a black man brought from
Africa by a white female Canadian anthropologist who'd finally
found love; she always locked him up naked in her apartment

in Ottawa whenever she went out so he'd never leave her!

The rain pouring again. Lightning, thunder. My down-town Ottawa bachelor apartment had a view from the balcony of Parliament Hill, cameras on tripods. Was there a deranged Lebanese holding up a bus once again? Sussex Drive: the heavily guarded prime minister's residence.

I will always try to be the model Canadian, mother. Always grateful for being accepted into the Promised Land with its ice and snow. I'd even take a long walk in the park from time to time during a blizzard. Oh, the future of Pierre Trudeau's Canada!

You never know: I could have been the Reverend Jim Jones standing by a loudspeaker, whip in hand — a Master of all Races, a US Congressman in a helicopter, TV cameras documenting disaster.

Ruinous ground; a jaguar following the scent. Who was left behind!

My mother saying, 'You see, Son, I am glad you lef'. We too backward here.'

My air-mailed copy of *The Berbice Times* announced the race. Competitors were invited, not just from Guyana but from the Caribbean and beyond – from as far as Miami, New York, Toronto to swim across the Berbice – which was wider than Lake Ontario. It didn't matter if you drowned, it was a once-in-a-lifetime experience. *Ex-patriots, all you who left for whatever reason, who only kept up your voting overseas, there are prizes galore to be won. Prove yourself!* Competitors were announced: Portuguese names, Syrians and others well-to-do: (Syrians: a catch-all for Jews, Arabs, whites); and a few blacks and browns: Alphonos, De Freitas, De Venterul, Aubrey. Where were Karran, Singh, Appadoo, Choudhary, Ali, Mohammed?

I now became one of the contestants; I, who regularly swam in the 'safe' public pools in Ottawa, who knew the 'scientific' method for the breaststroke, crawl and backstroke in my

demarcated lane of medium-fast swimmers. (How often I'd tag
along behind a shapely bikini-clad woman, doing my lengths).
But this was a challenge to a show of brute strength, courage;
waves lapping against my body; tangling with weeds, branches,
and fish swimming at cross purposes. Bramble bush, rhododen-
dron, mangrove; mosquitoes long as fingers. Wasps ready to
tear chunks of flesh from my neck and shoulders.

My mother and Auntie watching, exhorting.

The river was mudbrown, silt-clogged; fish mysteriously
scurried about or made false dives; the sun was high. I was
taking my time. In my mind's eye, that same deserted place,
mudcrabs scuttling about.

A boat alongside, how I gasped! The others were quickly
moving ahead. This was no indoor swimming-pool race. Mud-
clogged, leaf-laden, driftwood amid the silt-and-grime, I was
being pulled down to the river's bottom. 'Swim faster!' came a
cry. A kingfisher swooped, buffeted in the overhead wind.

I gasped for breath again. Was I really heading somewhere
far from Guyana? Past the islands, the blue sea, the aquamarine
haze. Such tranquillity? Past Cuba, Florida; kicking against the
mouths of sharks? Further south, heading for the Cape of Good
Hope. I suddenly held onto a large fish; I dolphined. I was
Vasco da Gama, no longer stuck on mud-ridden *Treasure
Island*, Ben-Gunned!

Where was I? Moving East? Making up for lost time in this
Middle Passage, my own caravel, a slave-ship, carrying me
along without astrolabe or quadrant. Only the heart's instinct,
without tide or stars. The hope growing, waves unending.

Then revulsion, as I swallowed weeds, algae, plankton. Was
I still heading for the subcontinent — far beyond Bermuda,
Africa, India? Auntie was watching me, laughing. My mother
too, eyes sunfilled. And Grandmother, looking on from the
balcony, filigreed, foot and nose rings her decoration. She was

always a sugar estate's maharajin.

'Swim on, you gon win!' I heard. But where was I? It wasn't just a simple race any longer. A whole crowd was swimming along. Was this a prelude to a collective drowning? Suicide perhaps the only route out? Jim Jones, do you hear? Zion, here I come... Alphonos, Aubreys, Singhs, Mohabirs: *class no longer matters!* Only the hustle, entrepreneurial busyness. Waves slapping, an entire ocean's boundaries marked out. Where were Surinam, Cayenne, Trinidad, Barbados, Antigua, Grenada, Aruba? All one long archipelago but no Caribbean Common Market or Federation. No access to a resource-rich hinterland. My mother laughing: 'Boy, is just a race!'

Auntie's *beata* raised, eyes gleaming despite the rain.

I swam harder, throwing arms, legs, a determined crawl, still gasping for breath. My mother and auntie kept applauding, despite Alphonso, De Venterul, Fernandes, Low-a-Chee. Bodies floating like dead fish; my eyes closed; the once-blaring radio now silent. Now I was in the middle of no man's land. My mother watched me, alarmed; Auntie watching, too, as I stretched out a hand to both of them; they holding on to me, gripping hard; pulling me out as if I was in real danger!

The headlines in the papers the next day: 'Failed Canadian swimmer!': the *Globe and Mail*. This was no Lake Ontario. I was delirious still. The unconquerable Berbice. Why had I thought it was no bigger than a Canadian lake? Who indeed could conquer such a river with all its stygian murk? The Berbice: well, it was the measure of all other rivers: the Mississippi, Mackenzie, Orinoco, Amazon, Ganges, Brahamaputra, Nile, Tigris, Euphrates, Thames, Seine, the Yangtse, Liffey, Rhine: rivers spawning a million creeks that fed mighty oceans and were in turn fed by them; rivers that swirled round the world: Frazer, St. Lawrence, Hudson. I was still swimming, desperately throwing my arms and legs in the breast stroke, all other strokes, learned-unlearned.

I sucked in air, feeling my heart's incessant palpitation.

The stelling was before me. I was standing firmly on it, my senses numb. I was laughing, looking back, intent on seeing all the other swimmers.

'Look, see!' I was telling my mother, Auntie, Grandmother, 'I came in first!'

Rubbing my eyes, it was Auntie not my mother I saw. Auntie, the clothes flapping on the barbed-wire wind. Water in my eyes; memory of ice, snow, sleet. My mother waving to me, wanting me to come back some day; the telephone's crackle of static. 'You must, eh!'

Auntie moaned, weathering the immigration official's barbs to live anywhere in this wide expanse of land: the Maritimes, Ontario, the Prairies, British Columbia, the Northern Territories — though not in Quebec. *Parlez-vous francais?*

My ancient corrugated grandmother slowly got up from the cowdung-plastered bottom-house. Heavy Northwestern Ontario winds blow across Lake Superior. She waves an indentured handkerchief, a time-hardened ethnic above all else!

Alone in the Ottawa streets of politicians, civil servants: familiar-unfamiliar looks. Are we talking about racial discrimination? Who was it said, 'A bigot's a rainbow without colours!'? On Parliament Hill a crowd was advocating gay rights in Canada.

Someone nudged me. I looked familiar to him; he wanted to know what I was doing here. Here was a new immigrant: Alphonso, De Venterul, Low-a-Chee, Wong? He'd heard of the Berbice river. Had I tried swimming across it?

Monty looked intently at me, the real Africa still in him, the Middle Passage's memory. He wanted to know all about that first slave rebellion.

I'm walking down these same Ottawa streets, the camera on a tripod steady on Parliament Hill. Who'll be the next prime minister? Who?

Now touching an Elijah Harper feather...

I began speaking softly, in the dialect of crossing.

METHUSELAH
for Jan Carew

Methuselah was going back to the trees in Northern Ontario.
Met, they called him. 'Met, boy — you there?' The question
came as he imagined being face to face with Nanabijou, the
Sleeping Giant. He was carrying on a conversation with this
Ojibway legend, the mountain rising up before him, Lake
Superior in the background. Nanabijou himself was speaking.
Met rubbed his eyes, awake now like Rip Van Winkle after all
these years, more than ten, to be exact, though it seemed much
longer. He'd planted thousands of trees in the wilderness at
Trapper Lake, Quetico, the region surrounding Lake Superior;
and he often recalled feeding the paper mills of Abitibi in
Thunder Bay itself. Yes, it had happened.

'I am here,' he proclaimed loudly, almost grandiloquently.

Laughter, the entire mountain laughing; and he too laughed,
as if a strange madness had taken hold of his mind.

Met listened to himself, he listened with a keenness he'd
never felt before. He recalled the hinterland of that far-away
place, the forest calls of birds, lizards and other reptiles; he'd
been haunted by them, and just when he thought he'd forgotten
it all, it now returned.

'You're with me now, Met,' the thunderous voice boomed in

the tympana of his ears.

'Am I' he asked, a little feebly.

'Yes, you're back there with me; I mean here. Remember the trees? See how they've grown: the spruce, jackpine, fir... they're all around. No power-saw can touch those trees; they have my protection. They inhabit the region like a lifeblood, and my people — you're one of them — are here, close to the trees, to the forest. It's the spirit you all find there, the spirit of all our ancestors.'

'All?'

'Yours and mine, Met.'

Met wasn't sure what to think, but as he listened to the hum of the lake, the wind and remembered the noises of the winter storms that only the North experienced, something else stirred in him, a sense that there was some commonness to all things. It dizzied him merely thinking about it. He put his hand to his head where he felt a throbbing and wished he could stop it.

Close by him Nanabijou muttered, 'You see, Met, I always wanted to tell you this, even before you came back here. Somehow I knew you'd be here with us. To plant these trees. To smell the closeness of the soil, the sand, the muskegs; breathe deeply as you did, alone in the forest with the blackflies and mosquitoes all around you. And the winos, the drunks, the men from Sioux Lookout and Longlac, grumbling, cursing about fights with the RCMP; you had to have them around you... I knew it was bound to happen. You had to be here. It was no more than a long sleep. Things have happened, you see. No mere imaginings.'

Met nodded, waking up further and looking about him. Where was he now? Some place. Not in no-man's land any longer. He was breathing heavily; he could feel the lake, feel it in his bones, as he had felt the coffee-coloured tropical rivers, the mudbanks with crawling alligators, the splash of reptiles hounding his dreams at night. Now he could hear again the noises of a winter storm, a howling like an elephant in distress.

Nanabijou was laughing. Met started laughing too. He liked what was happening now, the feeling of freedom in his spirit, though at the back of his mind he still wondered where he was. Something galvanised his spirit, something he'd never previously felt, not even while living there in the tropics; or here, with the other tree planters, even when they played cards late at night in the camps close to Lake MacKenzie in the heart of Quetico; even as they had talked boisterously all night long, even in their sleep; even while the lone one, Ojibway no doubt, walked in late at night, his heavy boots tramping on the heavy ground in the camp, throbbing like the recall of an ancient nightmare.

'You see, Met,' continued Nanabijou, taking him to a poolhall where the others from Thunder Bay, not far from the reservation, now whiled away their time. 'Not much has changed for the trees which you and the others planted. But look at them, watch them throwing darts; see how good they are at it, how they too are laughing. We must continue laughing — it's good for the spirit. All these years you've been silent. I didn't hear from you. You haven't been hearing me. Where were you? Ten years is a long time.'

'It's been longer than ten years.'

'Oh?'

'Aeons.'

'Yes, I know. Ancient time —'

'Or modern time.'

'Ah, what does it matter?'

'You're right, it doesn't. And place: here, there ... it doesn't really matter.'

But Nanabijou suddenly seemed aloof, for he was looking once more at the trees, as if they were part of the conversation, with their talking words amidst a shrill rustle from time to time,

waving their arms, gesticulating in the strong wind. Then
Nanabijou, good humoured as he was, started laughing again.

'Yes, you're right, Met; you've been around, young as you
are. Don't get me wrong, I've been accustomed to being in one
place all my life — well, mostly, so I'm accustomed to thinking
about place as if that was all. But there's spirit too. My people,
the Ojibways, have always made something of a fetish of it,
totem poles and all.'

Met now recalled the lone Ojibway walking into the camp
late at night when everyone else was asleep, his heavy boots
tramping like time itself. He was one who often preferred being
alone in the forest after he'd finished planting his trees, closing
his eyes and meditating like a Hindu. It had been more than
mere planting trees for him, Met realised.

The click of billiard balls, the concentration on the faces of
his old companions, the former winos, drunks, drifters, those
from Longlac and Sioux Lookout: they were all here now with
the self-importance of executives in a boardroom, engaged in
this act which consumed a good deal of their lives, which was
a ritual that enabled them to face and welcome each new day.
There was dignity in their concentration. No sound, no voice,
save for the humming thoughts; a little like trees themselves in
their individual expressions: the twitch of the lips, the curva-
ture of the dimple that rippled the stream of their cheeks, a new
thought flitting through the mind with quicksilver ease.

'Watch them good, Met; they're like the fellas back there too,
eh? The domino players — I've heard about them where you
come from. Yes, place makes no difference; it's time, that's all;
time bridges everything, divides everything too, brings all
things finally to one. Just think of it. You grow up and you will
realise the importance of time — not place, you see.'

Methuselah watched the dart players in the far corner: how
they aimed and threw with an easy deliberation peculiar to the
game.

Nanabijou looked in Met's direction, at how he too concentrated; but his eyes were rheumy, he couldn't concentrate for too long, not on something as specific as this. Yet the flight of a dart registered in his brain and kept him there, in this building which had somehow now become one of a febrile busyness.

'Wait a moment longer, Old Man of the Mountains; wait an' let's see what they're up to,' urged Methuselah.

'Yes, young as you are —'

'Indeed, young as I am.'

'But remember, one day you'll no longer be young.'

'I'm not that young, even now. Those trees have grown; I have grown with them.'

'Forgive me, I've made a mistake perhaps.'

'Yes —'

'Old as you are, thirty, forty. Ah, maybe you too have experienced it all.'

'But not imagined it all!'

'Right.'

There was a lull between them in the worn ramshackle building, the energy of the men's concentration being all that mattered now, all that seemed to exist. There were voices, mute voices in their ears, telling them to stay longer; voices of trees talking, whispering: the new inhabitants of the place.

Then suddenly, rapturous laughter: a white ball hitting the red and racing into the pocket. Time to call it quits! What else was there to do? Drink? What was there really to do? Go under a poplar and think. Yes, there we shall wait for the Great Spirit to come.

'I am here, Met,' said Nanabijou.

'Ah, I nearly forgot.'

'You must never forget. They never will, wherever they are.'

'I promise.'

... Wind and rain. Outside the constant battering in a tropical place. Voices. A ragged boy's steps, slip-slapping in the mud in what was much more than a game. More rain pouring down; tropical upheaval now; voices heard despite the thunder and criss-crossing lightning. Imagine being there, Nanabijou. Imagine time and place as one, and then crossing the barriers; imagine taking your people there as indentured workers, slaves. You cannot. It's a far sky; the wilderness and the hinterland will never be all.

'You must keep on promising to do what you believe.'

'I promise.'

'Once again, Met.'

'Your turn now.'

'I make this vow.'

'Will you lie on the mountain forever?'

'Maybe.'

'Whose territory?

'You ask that again?' Nanabijou coughed a little. 'All territory is ours, the same, eh?'

'I guess so. There, here... maybe; I will consider this too.'

'It's still a promise.'

'Agreed.'

More wind and rain, thunder, the dance of lightning in a perplexed sky in a time far away, a place distant and yet so very close.

In the wilderness, in the far paradise of close ranges, there is also flat ground. Ancient warriors, helmeted, tread through these same lands with false steps. Now more recent explorers are hacking their way through the trail with machetes, chopping at the vines, liana, slapping away at the mosquitoes and blackflies. A forest is always a forest, temperate or tropical.

Sleep now, on a bed on the mountain; sleep on flat land too, if you like; on the surface of Lake Superior. Then, Met says to

himself, together we will rise up; and he recalled promises of
ancient times, promises built on codes, laws, dicta of human
rights — all attempting to refurbish a life when the past and
present were really one, without strife.

Also by Cyril Dabydeen:

The Wizard Swami
Cyril Dabydeen

When Devan, the awkward boy from Providence Village, finds his vocation as a teacher of Hinduism to the rural Indians of the Corentyne Coast of Guyana, his life and his troubles begin. In this richly comic novel, Cyril Dabydeen creates a vibrant picture of the Guyanese Hindu community struggling for a place in what for Devan is a confusingly multiracial country. In the tragicomic absurdities of Devan's career, Dabydeen reveals the dangers to a religion's truths when it is made to serve the needs of ethnic assertion. But in becoming the Wizard Swami, in charge of Mr. Bhairam's prize racehorse, Destiny, Devan not only reaches his lowest point, but begins to discover truths of a far more tentative but enlightening kind...

ISBN 0 948833 19 X
£4.50

Dark Swirl
Cyril Dabydeen

When a European naturalist arrives in a remote South American village, how are the villagers to respond to his promise to remove the monstrous massacouraman from the creek? Is he a saviour freeing them from its danger, or is he threatening to take away something which is uniquely theirs for display in an American or European zoo?

ISBN 0 948833 20 3
£4.50

Peepal Tree Favourites:

Cosmic Dance
Harischandra Khemraj

Dr. Vayu Sampat is brought two stories: the rape of a young girl by a powerful state official, and a seemingly altruistic gift of blood. The first is an all too common event, the second all too rare in a society where the strong feed off the weak, and everything has it's price.

Cosmic Dance is a gripping and thought-provoking read. A fast-moving and bloody political thriller, it deals acutely with the issues of race and gender in modern Guyana, and the interplay between intention and chance in human affairs. Unmissable.

ISBN 0948833 45 9
£6.95

Timepiece
Jan Shinebourne

Sandra Yansen leaves behind the close ties of family and village when she takes a job as a reporter in Georgetown. The novel explores the connections between personal and political integrity in a society where people 'break up the ground under each others' feet', and reflects sensitively on the position of women in Guyanese society.

'This is not a novel to be taken at face value for its joy lies in the fact that it works on so many different levels... the subtleties and tensions of life are not far from the surface as the author questions the notions of political as well as individual dependence and independence.' *Spare Rib*

ISBN 0948833 03 3
£4.50

Peepal Tree has over 70 titles in print, from Caribbean, South Asian and Black British authors. We publish fiction, poetry, children's books, history and literary criticism. Write, phone or fax us for a **free** copy of our catalogue.

All Peepal Tree books should be available through your local bookshop, if you have any trouble finding them, please contact our orders department direct, and your books will be despatched within 14 days. If, for any reason you are unhappy with a Peepal Tree book ordered direct from us, we will be happy to refund your money.

You can contact Peepal Tree at:
17 King's Avenue
Leeds LS6 1QS
United Kingdom
***tel* 0113 2451703**
***fax* 0113 2468368**

When ordering books direct, please enclose a cheque or postal order for the cover price , plus 50p towards postage and packing. Overseas customers may pay in sterling, US or Canadian $, but please add £1.00, $1.00 or $1.50 respectively for shipping.

About the Author

Cyril Dabydeen was born in the Canje district in Guyana, South America. His grandfather, popularly known as 'Albion Driver', moved to the Rose Hall sugar estate where Dabydeen grew up and attended, and later taught at, the St. Patrick's Anglican school. He finished his formal education at Queen's University in Canada. He has done an assortment of work; mainly taught at Alonquin College and at the University of Ottawa. He also works in race relations. His books of poetry include: *Poems in Recession* (1972), *Distances* (1977), *Goatsong* (1977), *Heart's Frame* (1979), *This Planet Earth* (1979), *Still Close to the Island* (1980), *Elephants Make Good Stepladders* (1982), *Islands Lovelier than a Vision* (Peepal Tree, 1986) and *Coastland* (1989). He has published three collections of short stories, *Still Close to the Island* (1980) *To Monkey Jungle* (1988) and *Berbice Crossing* (Peepal Tree, 1996) and two novels, *Dark Swirl* (Peepal Tree, 1989) and *The Wizard Swami* (Peepal Tree, 1990).